THE TIME OF THE WITCH

MARY DOWNING HAHN'S fascination with the mysterious beauty of the West Virginia hills, and her own experiences as a divorced mother, led her to write *The Time of the Witch*. Previously a junior high school art teacher and English teacher at the University of Maryland, Ms. Hahn now works as a children's librarian. She lives with her husband in Columbia, Maryland, which she says is "a town too new and well-polished to harbor a witch as obvious as Maude."

THE TIME OF THE WITCH

MARY DOWNING HAHN

AN AVON  CAMELOT BOOK

To my family

AVON BOOKS
A division of
The Hearst Corporation
1350 Avenue of the Americas
New York, New York 10019

First Avon Camelot Printing: September 1991

CAMELOT TRADEMARK REG. U.S. PAT. OFF. AND IN OTHER COUNTRIES, MARCA
REGISTRADA, HECHO EN U.S.A.

Printed in the U.S.A.

OPM 10 9 8 7 6 5 4 3

chapter

-<1>-

"Are we almost there?" Jason asked for at least the millionth time.

Mom nodded. "You'll see the house as soon as we get to the top of this hill."

Angrily I slumped down in the seat, staring at the back of Mom's head. Why should I care what the house looked like? All I wanted to see was our own house in Stoneleigh, now hundreds of miles away, not my Aunt Grace's dumb old house in the middle of West Virginia. "Get your thumb out of your mouth," I hissed at Jason, giving him a nudge intended to jar his thumb loose.

"Laura," Mom said, giving me a warning look in the rear view mirror, "get over on your side of the seat and leave Jason alone!"

She shifted to a lower gear and kept the car going uphill, despite the rain and mud. Glancing out my window, I saw the ground drop straight away from the edge of the road, down, down, down, into a valley I couldn't see the bottom of. Shuddering, I slid back across the seat toward Jason and looked out his window at the steep side of a mountain rising up into the cloudy sky.

1

What an awful place. Dirt roads, no houses for miles, a total wilderness. How could my aunt enjoy living in a place like this? And how was I going to stand a whole summer of it?

Remembering the tree-lined streets of Stoneleigh, the well-kept brick houses, the wide green lawns, I felt so homesick I wanted to cry. But not here, not with my five-year-old brother Jason sitting next to me sucking his thumb, not with Mom peering through the windshield, using all her skill not to send us hurtling off the road and into that valley. I wanted to cry in private.

"There it is!" Mom pointed and without much enthusiasm I looked across a valley at the house.

It was a big stone house, dark gray in the rain, sitting high on the crest of a hill. The lawn around it was a deep green and behind it rose the Blue Ridge Mountains, veiled with clouds. It was a beautiful place for someone who likes scenery and nature and peace and quiet, but I could tell at a glance that there wasn't going to be a thing for me to do all summer.

We dipped down the hill and turned into the driveway, climbing steeply up toward the house. I was sure Mom would stall the car, but somehow she managed to get us to the top. Skidding to a stop, she cried, "Grace!" and leaped out of the car to meet her sister.

I looked out the window at a red-haired woman dressed in faded jeans hopping barefoot through the puddles, a big grin on her face. The two of them threw their arms around each other, laughing like people in a TV commercial while Jason and I sat in the car like two forgotten suitcases.

"Laura! Jason!" Mom turned to us smiling, "Come on out and meet your aunt!"

2

"It's raining," Jason whined.

"Well, you won't melt, silly. We'll run right into the kitchen and dry off." Mom opened the car door, still smiling, her hair dark with rain and sticking in little ringlets to her face.

"Go on." I shoved Jason. "I can't get out till you get out." With her usual skill, Mom had pulled up right next to a big wet bush, and I knew I'd get soaked if I opened my door.

"Don't push me, Laurie!" Jason turned toward me, his face angry.

"Why not?" I gave him another shove, a little harder this time, and he slapped my arm.

Before the fight could really get going, Mom grabbed Jason's arm and pulled him out of the car. "Please don't fight," she said softly. "What will Grace think of you?"

"She pushed me," Jason said, his voice shrill.

"Laura, leave him alone. I *mean* it," Mom said, blaming me as usual for everything.

By this time, Aunt Grace had opened the trunk and grabbed a couple of suitcases. "Laura, can you get the other two?" she asked as I got out of the car.

Without a word, I took the suitcases and followed her up the back steps and into a big, old-fashioned kitchen.

"Just leave the suitcases in the hall for now. I've got water boiling for tea." Aunt Grace busied herself at the stove and the rest of us sat down at a big oak table.

While we drank tea, Mom and Aunt Grace did most of the talking, remembering every now and then to ask Jason and me a question, usually something boring about school or what we liked to do. Because there wasn't anything better to do, I listened to them talk about the summers they'd spent here when they were children, when their grandmother (my *great*-grand-mother) was alive.

"She was a wonderful old lady, wasn't she?" Mom smiled at Aunt Grace. "I wish she'd lived long enough for you to know her, Laura."

"Poor Laura, she never even knew her own grand-mother, let alone her great-grandmother," Aunt Grace said.

She and Mom looked at each other and I knew they were feeling a little sad. Their mother had died when Mom was two and Aunt Grace was seven, so Mom re-membered her grandmother better than she remem-bered her own mother.

"Do you really like living here, Grace?" Mom asked, forgetting about me again.

Aunt Grace nodded. "It's wonderful. I don't miss New York a bit. These past five years have been the best of my life."

"But don't you get lonely?" Mom glanced at the big bay window that looked out toward the mountains. "There's no one around for miles and you're all alone."

I could tell by Mom's tone of voice that she would find it scary living here without any neighbors and I looked at Aunt Grace, waiting for her answer.

She smiled and shrugged. "You get used to it, An-drea. And I'm painting better than ever up here. Want to see my latest?"

Mom followed Aunt Grace to a corner of the kitchen set up like an artist's studio. In front of the bay win-dow stood a large drawing table and against the wall was a set of shelves that held a variety of paints and brushes, pens and ink, and stacks of paper. A fat ginger cat looked up from the window seat and twitched his

4

tail warningly at Jason while Mom leaned over the table to admire an unfinished painting of a crow perched on a dead tree. It was very well done, right down to the gleam in the crow's eye, but it was sort of eerie. The crow had a sinister look and the stormy sky behind him was ominous.

While Mom oohed and aahed, Aunt Grace showed her a stack of paintings of birds and animals and ferns and rocks and trees. They reminded me of Andrew Wyeth's paintings, very realistic but somehow weird and mysterious at the same time, as if there were things going on under the leaves or in the shadows that you wouldn't want to know about.

"These are wonderful, Grace," Mom said. "I wish I had a tenth of your talent."

Aunt Grace smiled and pushed her hair out of her face. "Well, I enjoy painting them, so I'm glad to find people who enjoy looking at them. Luckily there seem to be enough of those to help me earn my living."

Mom turned back to the crow and frowned. "This one is the only one I don't particularly care for. I never have liked crows." She paused and then added, "I guess it reminds me of someone I'd rather forget."

Aunt Grace nodded. "I know. I think I had her in mind when I painted it." She cocked her head to one side, a little like a crow herself, and stared at the picture. "It makes me a little uneasy myself." She chuckled as if she weren't quite serious.

"Is she still around?" Mom asked.

"I see her once in a while, but . . ." Aunt Grace shrugged her shoulders and busied herself with the strings on her portfolio.

"Who?" I asked. Immediately I realized I should have

kept quiet. They exchanged looks that clearly said they'd forgotten a twelve-year-old was standing there listening.

"Oh, nobody," Mom said in this evasive tone of voice she uses when she doesn't want to discuss something.

"Just an old woman we used to know," Aunt Grace added, straightening up the paints and brushes on her art table.

Although I was sure they were deliberately keeping something from me, I didn't feel like pursuing it. After all, I wasn't particularly interested in old women or crows.

I walked over to the window, ignoring Jason and the cat. It was still raining and I was sure I'd never seen a drearier view. Aunt Grace's yard stretched away, green and wet, bordered with flower beds and hedges, and beyond it was an empty field, then a woods, and then the mountains. Not another house in sight. Total desolation under a gray sky rapidly turning dark. How was I going to stand a whole summer here?

chapter

⊰2⊱

The first week at Aunt Grace's wasn't as bad as I thought it was going to be. Of course, that was because Mom was still there, and she and Aunt Grace kept us so busy sightseeing and swimming at Lake Charles and going on picnics that we didn't have time to be homesick. It seemed like a vacation, and I guess I kept hoping that Mom would change her mind and take Jason and me home with her when she went back to Stoneleigh.

As usual I was wrong. The day before she was supposed to leave, Mom made it clear that she was going and we were staying. As a result, I spent most of my time sulking in corners and refusing to talk to her. Jason, on the other hand, sat on her lap, sucking his thumb and whining. But neither one of us had any luck convincing her that we were indispensable; more than likely, we had the opposite effect.

After she finally got Jason to bed, Mom came into my room and sat down on my bed, but I didn't look up from my Agatha Christie book. All day I'd been having fantasies about developing incurable cancer or drown-

7

ing in Lake Charles and imagining how horrible she'd feel when she drove up to West Virginia to get my body, knowing it was all her fault.

"You will look after Jason, won't you, Laura?" she asked softly. "I know you're angry at me for leaving you here, honey, but you'll have a great time. Grace is a wonderful person and this is such a beautiful place. I used to love spending my summers here."

Forgetting my plan to ignore her, I frowned at her over the top of my book. "Well, I'm not you," I said. "I'd rather be home in Stoneleigh, breathing polluted air at the swimming pool with my friends."

Mom sighed. "I can't take you back, Laura, you know I can't. I've signed up for three courses in both sessions of summer school, which means I'll be on campus every day and studying every night. Please try and cooperate. You know I need a good job."

"You wouldn't have to go to work if Daddy came back. You could go on just the way you always have, staying home and taking care of Jason and me. I don't want you getting a job and being gone all the time. I want you at home where you're supposed to be!" I threw my book down and glared at her. "I want you to stay married!"

"Laura, accept the facts. Daddy isn't coming back and I'm getting a job." Mom sighed and reached out to stroke my hair, but I pulled away angrily. Her hand dropped down on the quilt and one finger traced the swirls of stitches. "I know you're not happy about the divorce, but there's nothing anyone can do to change it." Her voice pleaded with me to understand, but I slid deeper under the covers, still glaring at her. When she reached out to touch me again, I rolled over on my stomach.

"I want to go to sleep now," I said with my face in my pillow.

"Oh, Laura, please try to understand."

I didn't answer her, and after a while she got up. "Good night," she said softly. "I love you, Laura."

"Mmmmh," I mumbled, pretending to be asleep.

Finally I heard her cross the floor and leave the room. I fell asleep listening to her and Aunt Grace talking in the kitchen. Their voices drifted up to me, muffled by the ceiling, but I caught a few works like "twelve is a difficult age," "she has to adjust," "doesn't understand," "she's insecure," and "unhappy." Enough to know they were talking about me. And that gave me a certain melancholy satisfaction.

Mom left early the next morning, and Jason cried all day. It was just horrible. Rain outside, tears inside, no television to watch, nothing on the radio but country music and static. By the time I went to bed, I'd never felt so depressed in my whole life. If the whole summer was going to be like this, I was sure I wouldn't survive till the end of August.

I couldn't have been asleep very long when something woke me up. Startled, I opened my eyes and saw Jason huddled at the foot of my bed.

"What are you doing in here?" I frowned at him, angry at being yanked out of a nice dream about the swimming pool.

"I had a bad dream, Laurie," he whimpered. "There was this big crow and it was chasing me and I was scared but I couldn't run and I couldn't scream and I was all alone in a big dark woods." As he talked, he crept closer to me, dragging his old teddy bear with him.

He looked so pathetic, I forgot about being angry. "It was just a dream, Jason. It wasn't real." I tried to sound comforting as he curled up next to me. "I won't let any old crow bother you."

He didn't say anything, but he looked up at me as if he were sizing up my ability to combat crows. "If Mommy was here, I wouldn't be scared," he said.

I shrugged, letting him know it didn't bother me to be a poor second to Mom. Then I remembered what I'd been thinking about before I fell asleep. Turning to Jason, I said, "Just suppose you had all the power in the world. Suppose you could do anything you wanted and everybody had to obey you. What would you do?"

"I could do anything?" Jason's eyes widened at the possibilities.

I nodded. "Anything. Like Aladdin when he rubbed the lamp and the genie came out, all huge and powerful."

Jason took a deep breath. "I'd have all the ice cream I could eat and a dirt bike and my very own color TV and lots of money and . . ." He gazed up at the ceiling, frowning slightly as he tried to think of more things. "What would you do, Laurie?" he asked.

"Make Mom and Dad love each other. Stop the divorce. Go back home to Stoneleigh and be a real family again."

"I didn't think of that." Jason smiled at me. "I'd make that happen too, Laurie. That would be the best thing in the world."

I leaned back against the tall oak headboard. Like everything else in Aunt Grace's house, the bed was an antique, and even though I'd been sleeping in it for a week, I was still worried that the headboard might come toppling down on me in the night and squash me like a bug under someone's shoe. Cringing away from it as it squeaked slightly, I smiled at Jason, forgiving him for his trivial wishes. After all, he was only five. "It would be wonderful, wouldn't it?"

Jason nodded. "Maybe when we go home, Daddy will be living with Mommy again and there won't be a divorce anymore."

Twirling a strand of hair around my finger, I shook my head. "I wouldn't count on it. The only reason Daddy ever came to our house was to see us, Jason. If we have to stay in West Virginia all summer, when will he and Mom see each other?"

Jason shrugged and snuggled closer to me. "Can I sleep in here tonight? I'm afraid that crow will come back, Laurie."

"I guess so. But just tonight," I added as Jason burrowed under the quilt, poking me with his cold feet.

"I know, just tonight, just this one night." He yawned and pressed his head against my shoulder. "Your bones are sharp," he said sleepily.

"So is your chin." I pushed him away and readjusted the covers, trying to keep out the cold air that crept in whenever one of us moved.

Before long, Jason was fast asleep, but I just couldn't relax. I lay there, tense as a stretched-out rubber band, watching the shadows of branches and leaves sway gently on the wall, willing myself to go to sleep. All around me, the house talked in its sleep. The stairs creaked as if ghosts glided up and down them, and the floorboards squeaked in response. In the hall downstairs, the grandfather's clock struck twelve long times and something thumped in the kitchen. I opened my eyes, tenser than before, trying to think of a logical explanation for the noise. It must have been the cat, I decided, jumping down from the table or knocking the trash can over looking for a little snack.

My eyes moved to the window. A crescent moon curved like a witch's smile against the dark sky and a mockingbird sang in a tree near the house, its voice sweet in the darkness. Hoping to see the bird, I slid quietly out of bed and stole to the window.

Shivering in the cold night air, I looked out, but I didn't see the bird. The narrow road below Aunt Grace's house lay empty in the moonlight. Beyond it, the ground dropped away into a valley and then rose again in hills toward the mountains curving against the starry sky. There was no light anywhere, and it scared me to look out into so much empty darkness.

Just as I was about to creep back to bed, I thought I saw something move in the shadows on the road. Curious, I watched until I saw a person step out into the moonlight almost directly beneath my window.

Drawing back, I stared at the old woman, afraid that she might see me. She lifted her face toward me and seemed to study the house, her eyes moving from window to window and stopping when they reached mine. For what seemed like a very long time, we stood staring at each other. Just when I thought I couldn't stand it anymore, she raised her hand in a strange gesture and turned away, leaning heavily on a tall walking stick.

For a few seconds, I stood still and watched her bent figure slowly disappear again into the shadows. Then I ran back to bed, shivering with cold.

As I pulled the covers over me, Jason stirred and

mumbled, and I snuggled up against him, grateful for the warmth of his body. I tried to forget about the old woman, tried not to think about what she might have been doing wandering around in the night, tried not to worry about the doors that Aunt Grace never locked.

chapter

~3~

When I woke up, I had the bed to myself. I could hear Jason prattling away to Aunt Grace in the kitchen, but I just lay there staring at the wall, not hungry enough to drag myself downstairs.

The wallpaper was very old-fashioned, a blue design on a beige background, repeating its patterns endlessly, and I liked looking for things in it. People, animals, birds; as in clouds, you could see all sorts of interesting things in the swirling, geometric shapes. This morning, though, it seemed to be full of old women. They stared at me from all sides, wrinkled and ugly, shaking their fists, leaning on walking sticks, making it impossible for me to enjoy staying in bed.

Not sure if I'd really seen the old woman outside the house, I got up and walked to the window. Like last night, the road was empty. Not a car, not a truck, not even a bicycle passed by, and it seemed highly unlikely that I'd really seen anyone there. After all, the nearest house was a mile away. Where could she have come from? It didn't make sense.

Opening a bureau drawer, I pulled out a T-shirt and

a pair of running shorts. As I was combing my hair, I heard Jason bellowing up the stairs.

"Laurie, breakfast is ready!"

"I'm not hungry!" I shouted back. I could smell bacon and pancakes, but it was already hot, too hot to eat anything.

By the time I sat down at the table, Aunt Grace and Jason were up to their ears in pancakes. "At last!" Aunt Grace smiled at me and started piling some onto a plate for me. "What would you like to drink? A big glass full of cold milk?"

My stomach lurched at the sight of all that food and the thought of milk. "I told Jason I wasn't hungry. All I want is a glass of orange juice and a cup of coffee." The pancakes were perfect, golden brown and lacy at the edges, but I shoved them across the table at Jason. "Here, you want them?"

He grinned, his mouth so full that syrup dribbled out the corners and ran down his chin. "Sure, I love pancakes."

Aunt Grace handed me the juice and coffee. "How about some cereal or toast?"

I shook my head. "This is all I ever eat for breakfast." I drank my juice and then my coffee, trying to ignore Jason. He was making faces at me, opening his mouth and shoving a mash of pancakes and syrup through his teeth, deliberately trying to make me sick. As I swallowed the last of my coffee, I pushed my chair away from the table and started to leave the kitchen.

"Laura, take your things to the sink and rinse them, please." Aunt Grace looked up at me from her drawing table. She said it pleasantly and she was smiling, but I knew she meant it.

Without a word, I picked up my mug and glass and ran water over them.

"What's written on the front of your T-shirt?" Aunt Grace peered at me, trying to read the fancy sparkly decal.

"It says, *I don't get mad, I get even.*" I looked down at my shirt and remembered the day I bought it. I'd gone to the mall with Kim, my best friend. We both had our baby-sitting money and we'd picked out T-shirts in a store where the salesgirl ironed any decal you wanted onto your shirt. Kim had picked out one that said, *Love is something special,* even though I'd told her it was sappy, and I'd gotten this one. Mom wanted to make me take it back, but they don't allow you to return things after they put on the decal, so I kept it. After all, I spent my own money on it. And I liked it.

"Is that your philosophy?" Aunt Grace looked at me curiously, as if she were trying to figure out what kind of person I was.

I shrugged. "Maybe." I was halfway to the door when I remembered the old woman. "I saw somebody in the road last night," I said. "An old lady. She was staring at the house. Do you know who she is?"

Aunt Grace dropped her eyes, a sure sign she wasn't going to be completely truthful. "It must have been Maude Blackthorne. She's the town eccentric. Perfectly harmless but a little crazy, you know? Every town has one."

"Not Stoneleigh. I've never seen anybody like that walk by our house."

"Oh, well, Stoneleigh." Aunt Grace shrugged, dismissing Stoneleigh. "It's too new to have a town eccentric."

16

"Does she live in Blue Hollow?" Blue Hollow, the nearest town, was at least five miles away. I couldn't imagine a woman that old walking five miles on a lonely road in the middle of the night.

"No, she lives up in the hills somewhere." Aunt Grace gestured vaguely toward the woods behind her house.

"Is she a total maniac or what?" I was getting more and more interested. Imagine living in a place where lunatics walked the roads at night. I could hardly wait to write a long letter to Kim, telling her all about the danger I was in. "She made weird gestures." I waved my fist, imitating the old woman.

"No, she's not a maniac, just a little eccentric like I said. Kind of nasty and spiteful, too. I'd steer clear of her if I were you."

I nodded and stole a glance at Jason. Just as I thought, he was sitting there, his fork halfway to his mouth, staring wide-eyed at Aunt Grace. "She's probably a witch who lures little kids to her house and eats them for dinner," I said, looking at Jason out of the corner of my eye.

"Don't be ridiculous, Laura!" Aunt Grace spoke so crossly that I stared at her in surprise. "She's just a pitiful, lonely old woman."

Jason slid off his chair and ran to Aunt Grace's side, his face worried. "There's no such thing as witches, is there?" he asked.

"Of course not, Jason. Laura was joking." Aunt Grace frowned at me over Jason's head. "Just forget about Maude," she said to me.

See what I mean? I'm always getting bawled out and blamed for every little thing. Without a word to either of them, I went out on the back porch, letting the screen door slam shut behind me.

17

But I didn't get to enjoy my privacy long. A couple of minutes later, the screen door slammed again and Jason sat down next to me, smiling and smelling as if he'd taken a bath in maple syrup. "What are you doing, Laurie?" he asked.

"Nothing." I stared at the mountains rising in the distance like a wall between me and Stoneleigh.

"Want to go down to the creek? Aunt Grace said we can."

I shrugged.

"It's cooler there." Jason scratched a mosquito bite on his leg. "We could build sand castles again."

Before I could say anything, I heard the screen door open. Aunt Grace smiled down at me. "That sounds like a great idea," she said. "It's supposed to go up to ninety this afternoon, and if I didn't have a picture to finish, I'd go with you and build a castle or two myself."

"Come on, Laurie." Jason tugged at my hand, anxious to go. Slowly I got up and allowed him to pull me across the lawn. Going to the creek with Jason was better than sitting around the house with Aunt Grace. Not much better, but still, as Jason said, it was cooler there.

"Don't forget what I told you," Aunt Grace called after us. "Stay on this side of the creek. The woods on the other side are tricky and you could get lost."

"We won't go in the woods," I promised, more to placate her than anything else. For some reason those woods looked interesting to me, and I planned to explore them someday. I was sure I wouldn't get lost. After all, I'd earned a woodcraft badge in Girl Scouts last year.

By the time we got to the creek, we were hot and sweaty from walking across the field in the sun. Taking off our shoes, we waded out into the water and splashed around, up to our knees in the deepest places.

"Look, Laurie." Jason held up a handful of dripping stones. "Don't they look pretty? They're like jewels, all shiny and bright and pink and yellow and silvery white. But when they're dry, they're just dull and tan and not pretty at all." He opened his fingers and let the stones fall in a glittering shower back into the water.

"I know. Seashells are like that too," I said. "Remember last summer when we went to Ocean City? We filled our buckets with shells, but when we took them back to the motel, they dried out, just like those stones, and they weren't pretty at all. Just broken pieces of old oyster shells, that's all they were."

"Daddy lived with us then, and he got mad at me because I was scared of the waves." Jason swirled one foot around in the water.

"Daddy just wanted you to be brave, Jasie."

Jason turned his back and walked farther downstream, kicking up a spray of water in front of him. When he was several yards away, he turned around, tears running down his face. "If I hadn't been scared of the waves and the deep end of the swimming pool and if I'd learned to play football and if I hadn't cried so much, Daddy would still live with us, Laurie!"

"It wasn't because of those things, Jason, it wasn't!" He looked so pitiful, I felt terrible. "Don't you remember that book from the library? It said children always think it's their fault, but it isn't. The divorce was between Mom and Dad, not us, Jason!"

"Books are wrong sometimes," he said. "I wasn't tough like Daddy wanted me to be and that's why he left."

19

I shook my head. "Come on, let's build a sand castle, okay?"

"Okay," he mumbled, wiping his eyes on the sleeve of his T-shirt. He waded slowly back to the strip of sandy gravel we called our beach and squatted down next to me. "Do you really mean that?" he asked, still looking pretty weepy.

I nodded. "You didn't have anything to do with it." I patted his arm in a motherly way and smiled at him. "Now come on, let's see how big a castle you can make."

For a long time, we squatted side by side shaping castles out of damp sand. All around us, birds sang in the woods. The shadows from the trees stretched over us, dappling everything with greenish light, and the creek chattered away to itself as it ran over the stones, sparkling in the sunlight. It was so peaceful that I forgot about everything except my castle.

I was just finishing up my third tower, when I started getting a funny feeling. Looking over my shoulder, I expected to see Aunt Grace standing behind me watching me, but I didn't see anyone. Just the creek and the trees and the clouds in the sky.

"What's the matter?" Jason looked up at me. "Are you finished?"

I didn't want to scare him, so I didn't say anything about my feeling that someone was watching us. "It's getting awfully hot," I said. And it was. The sun had moved overhead, chasing the shade back into the woods. My T-shirt was sticking to my back and my hair was a hot weight on the nape of my neck. On top of the heat, every mosquito for miles around had decided I was a gourmet's delight. "Let's go for a walk or something, wade up the creek where it's shady."

"I want to stay here," Jason said.

Jumping up, I shoved my foot through my castle. My towers crumbled and fell, and I smoothed the rest of it flat with my foot.

"Why did you do that?" Jason asked.

"It was a dumb castle and I was tired of it. Come on, let's do something else."

"No, I want to finish my castle." Jason squatted next to his castle, pouting.

I shoved my foot toward his walls. "Rummm, rummm, rummm," I said, making a rumbling engine sound. "Here comes the urban renewal bulldozer."

"No, Laurie!" Scuttling sidewise like a little crab, Jason thrust himself between me and his castle. "Stop it, Laurie! Don't wreck it!"

"Rummm, rummm, rummm." My foot grazed Jason's leg, gritty with sand. "Rummm, rummm, rummm!"

"Please, Laurie, please, it's my best castle!" Tears started spouting out of Jason's eyes the way they do in cartoons.

Feeling like a rotten bully, I stared down at him. "If I promise not to wreck your castle, will you go for a walk with me?"

"That's not fair. I don't want to go for a walk."

"Urban renewal is never fair," I said, remembering hearing Dad tell Mom something like that during an argument. "Life's never fair." I wiggled my foot under his leg, heading toward the castle again.

"Okay, okay!" Jason crouched next to his castle, his face red with anger. "But you better promise not to wreck it."

"I promise, Jasie. When we get back, I'll even help you dig a moat around it. How about that?"

Jason got up slowly, brushing his sandy hands on the seat of his shorts. "Which way are we going?"

"How about this way?" I pointed downstream and Jason followed me into the water, avoiding fallen branches and ducking under low-hanging bushes.

Picking up a leaf, I dropped it into the water. I watched the current snatch it up, whirl it around, and carry it away, whisking it past stones and hurrying it around snags. "Just think, Jason, if we were tiny, like Thumbelina, we could ride that leaf all the way to Washington, D.C."

"How do you know where this creek goes?" Jason scowled at me, still angry for being forced to leave his castle.

"Well, this creek dumps into a bigger stream and then a bigger one till it finally dumps into the Potomac River and the Potomac River goes right through Washington. You can see it from the top floor of Daddy's office building."

"I bet not many leaves get all the way to Washington." Jason pointed to a bunch of sticks jammed between two rocks. "See? Your leaf's already stuck."

I shrugged. "So? If we were riding on it, we'd steer around things like that."

Stepping over the snag, I splashed ahead of him, trying to ignore his whiny little voice complaining that I was walking too fast, that sharp stones were hurting his feet, that he wanted to go home. All of a sudden, I wanted to get away from him, from Aunt Grace, from all the safe sunny places where we usually played. I wanted to plunge into the wilderness and experience something strange; I wanted something to happen.

A movement in the leaves over my head caught my

attention. Looking up, I saw a crow perched on a limb curving over the water, his head turned toward me. He stared at me fearlessly, and I stopped, ankle deep in the creek, afraid to move until he flew away.

After a few seconds, the crow cawed loudly, still looking at me, and launched himself into the air. Without knowing why, I splashed after him, trying to keep his dark shape in sight.

chapter

⊰4⊱

"It's getting too deep, Laurie," Jason whimpered. "I'm scared I'll slip and fall."

Up to my own knees in swirling brown water, I looked back at Jason. The creek had narrowed. On one side, a wall of rocks rose up steeply and on the other the bank was much higher than it had been. The jolly sound the water had made as it ran rapidly over pebbles in the sunlight had deepened into a melancholy gurgle.

"Let's go back," Jason pleaded. "I don't like it here. It's scary."

I looked across the stream. At the top of the bank I could see a path. "Why don't we climb up there and follow that path back? I'm tired of wading."

Jason looked worried. "Aunt Grace said we weren't supposed to cross the creek."

"So? She isn't here to see us, is she? And, anyway, she's not our mother. We don't have to do everything she tells us."

"But we might get lost." By now Jason was standing next to me, plucking at my shorts with one hand.

"How can we get lost? The path follows the creek.

24

Come on, Jason, my feet feel absolutely waterlogged. Look, they're all wrinkly, the way they get if you stay in the bathtub too long." I held up one foot and almost lost my balance. "Besides, this water is freezing cold."

To my relief, he followed me across the creek and I helped him climb up the bank. Just as I thought, the path wound along the creek, curving around tall pines and outcroppings of rock, barely wide enough for one person to walk on. With Jason behind me, I felt like an Indian scout creeping through the forest.

"This is a scary place," Jason whispered, stepping on my heels in his eagerness to keep up with me. "It makes me think of Hansel and Gretel. Are you sure we won't get lost?"

"Of course we won't get lost. Look, the creek's right there." I looked down at the water frothing along between the rocks and I felt uneasy, just the way I had when we were building our castles.

All around us, the pines rose tall and straight toward the sky, blocking out the sunlight, carpeting the ground with a cushion of brown needles. Here and there, between the trees, rocks shoved their way out of the earth, towering over our heads. Like trolls turned to stone, the rocks had a watchful quality, as if they were silently waiting for someone or something to bring them back to life.

I looked all around, trying to see if anyone was following us, but all I saw was a crow, perched on the limb of a pine tree over my head. His yellow eyes reminded me of Aunt Grace's painting and I made a shooing motion at him, willing him to fly away.

"What was that?" Jason grabbed my arm and I jumped, startled.

"What?" I stood so still I could hear my heart pounding.

"I thought I heard something behind us." Jason clung to my hand, staring over his shoulder.

"It was probably a squirrel or a bird." I looked around, hoping I'd see a squirrel dash up a tree trunk. "Where did you hear it?"

"Over there." He pointed off into the woods behind us, at a boulder rising out of a bed of fern, its face bearded with moss and spotted with lichen.

"Come on." I grabbed his hand and yanked him along behind me. I wanted to get back to Aunt Grace's house.

"Well, well, well, who have we here?" An old woman wearing a strange assortment of mismatched clothing stepped out of the woods ahead, blocking the path. Like a cat ready to pounce, she stared at us, leaning her weight on a walking stick that was almost as tall as she was.

Holding Jason's hand tightly, I stood still, trying to look her in the eye. "Good afternoon," I said, as politely as I could. I wanted to run past her, but my legs felt like boiled spaghetti, so I just stood there, staring at her, sure she was Maude Blackthorne and probably a raving maniac capable of anything.

"I know who you must be," she said, stepping closer to us. "I'd know that red hair anywhere. You must be Margaret's granddaughter. Laura, isn't it? Staying with your Aunt Grace for the summer."

This close, I could smell the musty odor of old clothes. Shrinking back against Jason, I nodded my head. "How do you know my name?"

The old woman chuckled softly. "I know many things, Laura. Would you ask the moon how it knows the night's secrets? Or the roots of a tree how it knows the dark? I've seen you and Jason at the creek building your little castles and I've seen you sitting on Grace's porch in the evenings. Haven't you seen me, my dear?"

"On the road last night, I saw you then," I whispered.

"Ah, did you? I thought you might have, I thought it was your face at the window staring out at me."

"What were you doing there in the middle of the night?"

Maude chuckled again. "Walking about, walking about, up and down and round and round, enjoying the dark." Before I could duck away, Maude's hand shot out and grasped a few strands of my hair. "Such pretty hair, red like your grandmother's, long and wavy like hers. And your eyes, big and gray like hers. Pretty, pretty face like hers. Yes, seeing you brings back memories, memories of days when Margaret and I roamed these woods like sisters."

"We have to go." I backed away with Jason clinging to me. "It's time for lunch and Aunt Grace must be looking for us."

"What's this, Laura?" Maude leaned closer, staring at my T-shirt. "*I don't get mad, I get even,*" she crooned, tracing the words lightly with a long, jagged fingernail.

I drew back and folded my arms across my chest, wanting, too late, to hide my decal. "I bought it for a joke, to shock my mother," I said nervously.

Maude chuckled. "A joke, eh? I find it a rather interesting statement, my dear, one I quite agree with. Why, if I weren't such an old lady I'd go out and buy one myself."

27

She reached out and stroked my hair, untangling it with her strong fingers. "You must come to see me, Laura. I get lonely with no one to talk to. Your grandmother and I were such good friends, such dear friends. Please promise you'll come to see me. I live up there—see where the path goes?"

She pointed at a path so narrow I wouldn't have seen it without her help. "My little house is up at the top of the hill. There's not another house in sight, you can't miss it."

"I don't know," I stammered. I didn't want to hurt her feelings by saying no, but I certainly didn't want to go anywhere near her house.

"I'll make it worth your while," Maude said, bending so close to me I could see the pores in her wrinkled skin. "You see, I can help you, Laura. I know what you want and I can help you get it. I have the power to grant your wishes."

She leaned on her walking stick, her eyes probing mine as if she could read every thought hidden in their depths. "Come to me soon, Laura. I'll be waiting for you. In dark or in daylight, come to me and I'll help you for the sake of my old friend Margaret." Turning away, she struck off into the woods without looking back.

For a second, Jason and I stood still, staring at each other. Overhead, a crow cawed loudly and flew past us, taking the same direction as Maude.

"What did she mean, Laurie?" Jason looked up at me, his eyes huge.

"I'm not sure." I stared up the path after Maude, but she was already out of sight. Not a leaf rustled to mark her passing, not a branch stirred.

"You won't go to her house, will you?" Jason's voice trembled. "I'm afraid of her. She's not nice, I can tell."

"Come on, let's go back to Aunt Grace's." I didn't need to make that suggestion twice. For once, I had to hurry to catch up with Jason.

By the time we got home, we were almost dead from the heat and out of breath from running. Before we went inside, though, I grabbed Jason's arm and leaned down so I could look him right in the eye. "Don't tell Aunt Grace about seeing Maude, okay?"

"Why not?" Jason squirmed, trying to get away from me, but I squeezed his arm tighter.

"She told us not to cross the creek, remember? She'll punish us if she finds out we disobeyed her. You don't want to get a spanking, do you?"

Jason shook his head, his lip trembling. "No."

"Then keep your mouth shut about Maude. I mean it, Jason." I gave him a little shake and then released him so quickly he lost his balance and sat down in the grass. "Come on," I said, "let's go in and have lunch. I'm starved."

After lunch, Jason fell asleep on the living room couch and I sat down on a stool near Aunt Grace's drawing table to watch her paint. She was finishing up the crow, concentrating on adding highlights to his features. Sitting there looking at the painting, I realized whom it must have reminded my mother of. Maude, of course. Hadn't that crow followed her up the path like a dog following its owner?

Despite the afternoon heat, I shivered, remembering how often I'd seen a crow perched near Jason and me at the creek. As the sound of bees droning about the flowers in the window box drifted into the kitchen, I thought of a book I'd read last year about witchcraft. In it, the author had said that a witch usually had a familiar in the shape of an animal or a bird, such as a toad, a cat, or a crow. If Maude were a witch, the strange things she'd said to me made sense.

"My, Laura, you look very preoccupied. Whatever are you thinking about?" Aunt Grace smiled at me as she swished her brush in a jar of water.

"Oh, nothing." I hesitated. "Looking at that crow reminded me of this witchcraft book I read. Do you believe in familiars and stuff like that?"

Aunt Grace smiled and shook her head. "No. I'm not the superstitious type. But up here you'll find people who take it quite seriously."

"Really? Did you ever know anyone who claimed to be a witch?" I thought I'd put that pretty subtly, so I leaned back and started doodling on a piece of scratch paper. I didn't want to look too interested in Aunt Grace's answer.

"Once I did," she said slowly, "but I never believed her." She got up and stepped away from her drawing table, staring at her picture critically. "How does he look to you, a little menacing?"

I nodded. "He's really good. And he looks scary, sort of like a familiar." I wanted to get her back on the subject.

"A familiar, huh?" That's just what your mother thought." Aunt Grace smiled and ruffled my hair.

"The old woman she was talking about was Maude, wasn't it?" Keeping my eyes on my doodling, I waited for her answer.

"Are you planning to be a detective when you grow

up? You certainly seem to have mastered the technique of asking questions whose answers you already know." Aunt Grace laughed and sat back down. "Yes, she was talking about Maude, and yes, Maude claims to be a witch, and no, I don't believe her. Now can we change the subject?"

"Why don't you believe her?"

"Because I'm a realistic person with a practical mind. If I ever see any real evidence that a person can cast a spell or summon up the devil or ride through the air on a broomstick, I may change my mind, but so far I haven't come across a shred of evidence. Now what would you like for dinner tonight? We could have tuna salad or fried chicken. Which appeals to you?"

That night I woke up around midnight. I expected to see Jason in my doorway, but the house was silent and there wasn't a sign of him. Wondering what woke me, I slipped silently out of bed and tiptoed to the window.

The road lay empty, silvery in the moonlight, but someone stood on the lawn as still as a statue, her face raised toward my window. It was Maude, a crow perched on her shoulder. Even though I was standing behind the curtains in the shadows at the edge of the window, she raised her hand. While I watched, too scared to move, she turned away and strode back to the road, her shoulders bent but her step sure.

chapter

⊰5⊱

"Laurie, there's someone there!" Jason grabbed my arm and pointed toward the creek.

I stopped behind Jason, my hand on his shoulder, and stared at the wall of bushes bordering the creek. Even though the sun was shining, I felt the hair on the back of my neck rise and for a moment I wished I hadn't persuaded Jason at breakfast to go to the creek. Maybe we should have stayed in the backyard the way he wanted to. Although I wanted to see Maude again, I was afraid to get involved with a witch. If I let her help me, would I lose my soul to the devil or something?

With Jason clutching at me, I tiptoed ahead, trying to peer through the bushes without being seen.

"It's Maude, it's Maude, I know it is," Jason whimpered.

But it wasn't Maude. It was a girl around my age, but skinnier and smaller. With her back turned to me, she was slowly and methodically trampling Jason's sand castle flat.

"What do you think you're doing?" I slid down the bank as the girl whirled around to face me.

"What's it to you?" Folding her pale, freckled arms across her skinny chest, she stared at me as if I were the trespasser. Her face was small and pointed, splattered with freckles, and her eyes were a brown so dark I could hardly see the pupils. Her hair was short and bushy curly, several shades redder than mine.

"Can't you see that sign?" I pointed to a faded No Trespassing sign, pocked with bullet holes and sagging from a tree trunk on the bank of the creek.

"Course I see it. You think I'm blind or something?" The girl stared at me.

"Well, this is my aunt's property and I'm telling you to get off it!" I shouted. "Just look what you did to my brother's castle!"

The girl shifted her weight from one foot to the other, investigating what was left of Jason's castle. Then she looked over my shoulder at Jason. "It sure isn't anything to cry about," she said to Jason. "How was I supposed to know it was a castle? It just looked like a plain old heap of sand to me." She shrugged and smoothed the sand with one bare foot.

"It's okay," Jason sniffed.

"It is not okay, Jason! She hasn't any right to come here and mess up things on Aunt Grace's property!" I wanted to grab the girl by the straps of her overalls and shake her for standing there looking so smug. Who did she think she was?

"Well, what are you going to do? Call the cops?" The girl glared at me and then grinned at Jason, a friendly gap-toothed grin that squeezed her freckles together. "Hey, you want to build it up again? I'll help you."

Jason looked up at me without releasing his grip on my hand.

"What's your name?" I asked, still trying to sound as if I were in control of the situation.

"Wanda Orton." She grinned at me then. "What's yours?"

"Laura Adams. And this is my brother Jason."

"I got two brothers, but Billy's in the Marines and Duane's in the Army. Billy's in North Carolina and Duane's in Korea. I also got a sister Charlene. She works in Harrisburg at the Dairy Queen, but she lives at home still." Wanda paused, for breath I guess, and squatted on the sand next to Jason. "You want me to help now?"

Jason didn't look at her and he shifted toward the left, away from Wanda, but he nodded his head. "Okay," he mumbled.

Wanda started building up a tower she'd squashed flat. "You just visiting here for a while?" she asked me.

"We'll be here all summer." I knelt down beside her and scooped up some sand for another tower.

"Our mother and father are getting a divorce," Jason said, "so they can't take care of us now."

Wanda sighed. "That happened to me too. First my daddy ran off with a waitress at the Dew Drop Inn and then my mother went and left us with our grandmother while she went off to find a job."

Wanda paused and scrutinized her tower. "It's lop-sided, ain't it?" She patted it carefully back into shape. "She never came back, so my grandmother got stuck with all four of us and just when she finally got rid of Billy and Duane, Charlene went and had a baby and now she's got it to take care of too. She fusses about things sometimes, but I can tell she loves Tanya Marie."

"Does Charlene's husband live at your house too?" I

34

stared at Wanda, trying to make sense of what she'd said.

"Husband?" Wanda pushed her hair back from her forehead and laughed. "Who said anything about a husband? Charlene ain't married! Eddie ran off and left her when she told him she was pregnant and she hasn't seen him since."

I looked down at the sand, too embarrassed to look at Wanda. If I had a sister like Charlene I certainly wouldn't go around telling perfect strangers her life story.

"Does your grandmother have long white hair?" Jason asked.

Wanda stared at him, a little surprised at the sudden change of subject. She shook her head. "She's always saying she should have it from all the problems she's had, but her hair's redder than mine. Why?"

"We saw an old lady in the woods up there." Jason pointed across the creek. "She had long white hair and she looked like a witch."

"You must've seen Maude." Wanda's eyes widened and she looked in the direction Jason pointed, as if she were afraid the old woman was standing there watching us. "You know what people say about her, don't you?"

I nodded, my skin creeping. "My aunt says it isn't true, though. She says Maude's just the town eccentric."

"Ask my grandmother about her sometime. She'll tell you she's a witch all right." Wanda hunched over the castle, her body tense.

"You said she wasn't, Laurie. You said she wouldn't hurt us." Jason stared at me, his lower lip trembling.

35

"Well, I can tell you she is a witch," Wanda said, "And I wouldn't go anywhere near her or her house if I was you."

Jason put his hands over his ears and started singing the "Sesame Street" theme song.

"What's he doing?" Wanda stared at Jason.

"He always does that when he doesn't want to hear something scary. Don't pay any attention to him." I scooted a little closer to Wanda. "What do you know about Maude? How do you know she's a witch?"

"Well, she lives all by herself and she doesn't have anything to do with anybody. The only time she ever goes into Blue Hollow is to buy groceries. She doesn't even go to church. And she acts so peculiar. Comes down the road leaning on her walking stick in her dirty old clothes with that crow on her shoulder, mumbling and muttering and talking to herself, looking all around with mean old eyes, just waiting for a chance to say something nasty. I'm scared to death of her." Wanda paused to scratch a mosquito bite.

"Does she cast spells or anything?" I whispered.

"My grandmother claims she does. She says Maude can cure diseases and tell the future too." Wanda looked across the creek at the green trees rising tall and silent. A crow cawed and flew slowly from one to another. "Don't those trees sometimes give you the feeling they're watching you?" she asked.

I nodded, remembering what Maude had said about seeing Jason and me playing here beside the creek.

"What did she do when you saw her?" Wanda looked at me curiously.

"Nothing, really. She grabbed my hair, like this." I held up a few strands of my hair. "And then she said I looked just like my grandmother."

"She didn't cuss you or swing that big stick of hers at you?"

I shook my head. "She was actually kind of friendly. She kept saying what good friends she and my grandmother had been and then she said I should come to see her, that she could help me." I stared at Wanda. "Even though she didn't do anything, she was scary."

Wanda nodded. "I wonder what she wants to help you with."

I shrugged. I didn't know Wanda well enough to tell her how badly I wanted to get my parents back together again.

"Charlene went to her once, but it didn't do her any good. She got a love potion or something to make Eddie marry her, but she's still waiting." Wanda stood up and brushed the sand off the seat of her overalls. "Well, it was nice meeting you all, but I got to get on home. It's about time for Tanya Marie to wake up from her afternoon nap and I have to entertain her while my grandmother watches the soaps on TV. Maybe I'll see you tomorrow, Laura."

"Wait a minute!" I scrambled up the path behind Wanda. "What do you mean Charlene got a love potion from Maude?"

Wanda grinned at me over her shoulder. "I haven't got time enough to explain it now. If I don't get home, my granny will kill me for sure. Come on over to my house tomorrow. Okay?"

"Where do you live?"

"The next house down the road from your aunt going away from Blue Hollow. You can't miss it. It sets up on a hill and it's white where there's still some paint left." Wanda turned her back and ran off into the woods, leaving the bushes swinging wildly in her wake.

"Let's go home now, Laurie." Jason got up from the sand, leaving his half-built castle behind him. "I don't like it here anymore!"

Above my head a crow cawed loudly and I looked up. There he was, only a foot or so above me, perched on a limb, his yellow eyes regarding me curiously. Without thinking, I picked up a stone and tossed it at him. I was never good at throwing, so the stone missed him completely, but at least he flew away, cawing as he flapped across the creek and into the woods.

chapter

~<6>~

When we got home, Aunt Grace was out in the garden picking peas. "Just the people I was hoping to see!" she called. "Come on over here and help me fill this bucket."

"I hate peas," Jason wailed, but he ran across the lawn to join her.

I followed him slowly, hating the hot sun on my back, hating the cloud of gnats circling my head, hating the thought of kneeling down in the dirt and picking peas. I wanted to sit in the shade and drink a glass of cold Coke and plan what I was going to do about Maude. Making no effort to be friendly or pleasant, I yanked a few pods off the vine and dumped them into the bucket.

"Are we going on a pea diet?" I scowled at Aunt Grace, thinking she'd already picked enough to feed an army of vegetarians.

"What's the trouble, Laura? Heat getting to you?" Aunt Grace pushed her hair out of her face. Although her own T-shirt was damp with perspiration and beads of sweat glistened on her forehead, she smiled as if she enjoyed the heat.

"I thought it was supposed to be cool in the mountains," I said. "I thought that was one of the great things about being up here in the middle of nowhere—you got away from the heat."

Aunt Grace shrugged. "This *is* awfully hot weather. I guess we're having a heat wave. At least it cools off at night. That's more than you can say for Washington."

"Yeah, but we have air-conditioners there." I frowned at her, squinting in the hot sun. "How come you didn't tell me there was a girl my age living right down the road?"

"Do you mean Wanda Orton?"

I nodded. "We met her at the creek today."

"She wrecked my castle," Jason said, "but then she helped me build it back up again."

"To tell you the truth, I didn't think you'd like Wanda." Aunt Grace swatted a mosquito and went on picking peas.

"Why not?"

"Well, I'm sure she's quite different from the girls you know in Stoneleigh."

"So? Just because she's different doesn't mean I wouldn't like her." It was true that I'd never known anyone like Wanda. I couldn't imagine her sitting on a bench in the mall with Kim and me, eating ice cream and watching the guys go by, or lying on a towel at the swimming pool listening to a portable radio, or experimenting with makeup samples at the drugstore. She just wouldn't fit into Stoneleigh at all.

But it was different up here. I didn't have to worry about what Kim or Lisa or Shari would think. I could be friends with anyone, even a skinny girl in baggy overalls. Things that were important in Stoneleigh just didn't matter here.

40

"Wanda's very nice," I said a little stiffly, surprised to realize that I wanted my aunt's approval. I didn't want her to think I was a shallow person, a little snob from the suburbs.

"Well, I'm glad to hear that." Aunt Grace smiled at me. "Summer will be more fun for you now that you have a friend. Have you met her family yet?"

"No, but she told me all about her mother and father leaving her with her grandmother and never coming back. Isn't that awful? What kind of parents would do something like that?"

Aunt Grace shook her head. "I don't know, Laura. Annabelle's a good woman, though, and she's done her best to provide a good home for those kids. She really loves them."

"That's a funny name for a grandmother, Annabelle. It sounds too young or something."

"Oh, it suits her, Laura. She's a real character." Aunt Grace smiled. "I really enjoy her, even though she's always giving me advice I don't take."

"Like what?" I stared at her puzzled. It was hard to imagine anyone having the nerve to give Aunt Grace advice. She seemed less in need of it than anyone I'd ever known.

"Oh, she thinks I should get out more, meet people, go places."

"Don't you ever want to? I mean don't you get bored sometimes?"

"Now you sound like your father. He's never understood why I left New York and came up here to live like a hermitess, as he puts it." She sat back on her heels and gazed into the distance, at the mountains and the sky beyond. "I love it here. The peace and quiet, the beauty of it. I had enough social life in New York. I'm happier here than I've ever been, Laura."

I looked at the mountains too, wishing I could enjoy them the way she did, but they still looked like a wall to me. On the other side of them was Stoneleigh and that was where I wanted to be, not here sweating away in Aunt Grace's vegetable garden. I sighed. "Maybe I'm just not old enough yet, maybe I haven't had enough social life."

Aunt Grace nodded. "You've got a point, Laura."

"Wanda's got a sister named Charlene," Jason said abruptly. "She works at the Dairy Queen and she's got a baby named Tanya Marie and she ain't got no husband." He stuffed a pea in his mouth and grinned, oozing a little green through his teeth.

Aunt Grace looked surprised. "She hasn't got a husband," she corrected him.

"That's right. I guess they got a divorce too, just like Wanda's mommy and daddy. And just like our mommy and daddy."

"I guess so." Aunt Grace got up. "I think we have enough peas. Why don't we go inside and see how the chicken's doing? You and Laura could probably use a tall glass of something cold to drink, and so could I."

Before I went to bed that night, I turned out my light and went to the window. Although I looked in both directions, I didn't see or hear anyone on the road. Just moonlight and shadows and a mockingbird singing somewhere. No sign of Maude. To be sure, I stood at the window until the cool night air made me shiver.

As I crawled into bed, thinking I was safe from her, I realized it was awfully early. Not even ten o'clock. Maybe after midnight, while I was sleeping, she would creep past the house again, staring at my window, waiting for me to come to her and ask her for help.

Sometime in the middle of the night, I did wake up, but it was Jason who woke me, not Maude.

"Laurie, Laurie," he whispered, plucking at the covers and trying to climb in next to me.

"What's the matter? Did you have another bad dream?" I moved over, letting him curl up next to me.

"It was about Maude. I dreamed she was chasing us in the woods. We ran and ran and I fell down. You just kept on running, Laurie, and I was trying to scream but I could only grunt and I tried to get up and run but I couldn't. Then she caught me and her fingernails were long and sharp and so were her teeth. She laughed and laughed and she picked me up and took me away. She put me in a cage and she told me I was hers forever and I couldn't move, I couldn't move at all. Mommy and Daddy were there too, but they were mad; they didn't want to be there in the cage with me. They thought it was all my fault."

He was crying and shivering, so I put my arms around him and hugged him. "There, there, Jasie, it was just a dream, don't cry. Nothing like that could ever happen. I wouldn't let Maude hurt you, I'd save you, Jasie."

"I'm so scared, Laurie, I'm so scared. I wish we were back home in Stoneleigh."

"I wish that too, Jasie." I hugged him again. "Do you want to sleep in here?"

"Yes." Jason pressed closer to me, snuffling in my ear. "You don't really think Maude is a witch, do you?"

"Of course not. Like Aunt Grace says, she's just a harmless old crackpot. She can't hurt anybody." I tried hard to sound convincing, but the more I thought about

43

it the more I believed that Maude really was a witch. Not the kind Jason had dreamed about, the wicked Baba Yaga sort of witch who ate little children, but a real witch who knew how to cast love spells and put hexes on people and tell the future and, most important, stop mothers and fathers from getting divorces.

"Are you asleep, Jason?" I whispered.

"No." He looked up at me, his face worried. "I was thinking about Wanda."

"Wanda?"

"Yes. I was remembering what she said about her father and mother. You don't think Mommy would just leave us here with Aunt Grace and never come back, do you?"

"Of course not." But, the truth was, I'd been worrying about that ever since Wanda had mentioned it. Suppose Mom decided it was a lot easier to live by herself? No more of our messes to clean up, no more fights to break up, no more worrying about getting a babysitter everytime she wanted to go somewhere. When I really thought about it, I wasn't sure she got much fun out of Jason's and my company.

I smiled at Jason and stroked the inside of his arm with my fingertips, the way Mom used to. "She loves us too much, Jasie. And so does Daddy. You wait, things will work out okay."

Hoping I was right, I caressed him till I felt his body relax. Then I lay there, gazing out the window at the moon, thinking to myself that I would definitely go to see Maude, no matter how scared I was. She said she would help me because of my grandmother and I knew I had to let her. There wasn't any other way.

chapter

‹ 7 ›

"Do you think *that's* Wanda's house?" Jason pointed at an old frame house perched on the hill above the road.

"You can't expect the whole world to look like Stoneleigh," I said, quoting something Aunt Grace had said to me on our first trip into Blue Hollow.

To tell the truth, I didn't like the looks of Wanda's house any more than Jason did, but I was trying to be open-minded. Wanda's grandmother was probably too old to do much work in the yard and maybe she couldn't afford to get the house painted or buy screens for the windows or fix the front steps. And the rusty truck without doors standing in the weeds like a half-sunk boat probably belonged to Billy or Duane.

Anyway it was all in how you looked at things. Take an artist, for instance. He might think this shabby old house with the paint peeling off was the perfect subject for a painting.

"Aunt Grace's house doesn't look like this," said Jason the Philistine.

And of course he was right. Our great-great-grand-

45

father had built Aunt Grace's house out of stones he cut himself and it was as perfect now as it was the day he built it. And the lawn surrounding it was as velvety green as any lawn in Stoneleigh.

"Well, do you want to stand here all day thinking nasty things about Wanda's house or do you want to go see her?" I asked him.

Jason looked ashamed. "I didn't mean anything bad about it. It just looks kind of tired."

Without another word, he followed me up the deeply rutted driveway. When we reached the top of the hill, three of the meanest, most vicious looking dogs I'd ever seen came running out from under the porch, barking and growling as if they hadn't eaten for a week.

"Don't run, Jason!" I screamed. "Stand absolutely still and don't let them know you're scared!"

I grabbed for him, praying Wanda would appear and call the dogs off before it was too late, but Jason was too fast for me. Before I could move, one of the dogs grabbed his shirt and pulled him down. Picking up a stick, I ran toward the two of them, screaming for help. Just as I whacked the dog as hard as I could, I heard someone yelling behind me. Snarling, the dogs backed away from us and skulked in the weeds near the truck.

"Are you all right?" I knelt down next to Jason and put my arms around him.

He was crying too hard to answer. His shirt was torn and both knees were bleeding from his fall, but I couldn't see any teeth marks anywhere.

"What are you kids doing? Where'd you come from?" A tall woman brushed me aside and examined Jason. "You're all right, boy. Chief didn't put a mark on you. Now you stop that crying, you hear? Just stop it right now and I'll take you up to the house and clean you up and fix you a nice cold glass of Kool-Aid. Would you like that?"

"Are you Wanda's grandmother?" I stared at the woman. I hadn't given much thought to how she might look, but most grandmothers I knew had gray hair, with maybe a blue rinse on it. Just as Wanda said, this grandmother had bright red hair, done up in a solid mass of tight curls all over her head, and she was wearing purple eye shadow and black mascara and frosty pink lipstick. But she was smiling over Jason's head at me and her pale blue eyes were soft and kind.

"I sure am. And you must be Laura, Grace Randall's niece." Wanda's grandmother smiled, revealing a gap as wide as Wanda's between her front teeth.

I nodded. "And that's Jason."

"Well, pleased to meet you both. Wanda told me all about you, but I clear forgot when those dogs started making such a fuss." She smiled again. "You can call me Annabelle, just like Wanda does. I don't like being called grandmother. Makes me feel old before my time and my time's coming soon enough, honey." She patted her curls and winked at me. "It ain't real no more, but it sure beats gray, don't you think?"

I smiled. "It looks pretty," I said, wondering how on earth I could call someone old enough to be my grandmother by her first name.

"Wanda's out in back somewheres working in the garden. Why don't you go find her while I take Jason inside and clean him up some?" Annabelle started up the drive, carrying Jason. "You don't need to worry about the dogs. They won't bother you now they know you."

Keeping an eye on the truck I'd seen the dogs run under, I followed the drive around to the back of the

47

house. Just as Annabelle had said, Wanda was squatting in the garden, her back to me, pulling up weeds. When she saw me, she wiped her hands on the seat of her shorts and grinned. "Why didn't you get here sooner? I'm just about done now. I could've used some help."

"Don't you go running off somewhere, Wanda," Annabelle called from a window. "I want you to take Tanya Marie outside for a while."

Wanda rolled her eyes up at the sky and sighed. "Sometimes I think I see more of that baby than Charlene does. If she was a baby duck, she'd think I was her mother for sure." Wanda pulled up a few more weeds and tossed them on the heap beside her. "Well, at least that's done for this week. You want to go in the house and get something to drink?"

I followed Wanda up the sagging back steps and into the kitchen, glad to be out of the sun. Not that the kitchen was any cooler. If anything, it was hotter, but at least it was shady.

"Be sure that screen door is shut!" Annabelle called from somewhere in the house.

"It's shut," Wanda answered, though why it mattered I didn't know. The screen was so full of holes it looked as if someone had used it for target practice, and swarms of flies were crawling all over the dirty plates on the kitchen table.

Trying not to notice the bowls crusty with dried cereal, the dirty cups and glasses, and the frying pan filled with half an inch of congealed grease, I watched Wanda open a cabinet and pull out two plastic tumblers. "You want Bugs Bunny or the Roadrunner?" She held up the glasses so I could see the pictures.

"I don't care."

"I'll have the Roadrunner then. It's my favorite." Opening the refrigerator, she got out a glass bottle and poured us each a grape Kool-Aid. "Charlene gets these glasses from the Dairy Queen. We got the whole set, but these are the only two clean right now."

I nodded, not sure what to say.

"Charlene says they're going to be collectors' items someday and we can have a yard sale and make a fortune on them. You think she's right?"

I shrugged. "Who knows? My mom's always seeing things in antique stores that she gave to the Salvation Army years ago. She's still upset about giving her whole collection of dolls away when she was thirteen."

"Guess you should just keep everything in case it's going to be valuable someday, only where would you put it all?"

"Wanda?" Annabelle appeared in the doorway with Jason at her side. She was holding a little girl wearing nothing but a diaper and a big smile. "Guess who's ready to go for a little walk?"

"Come on, Tanya Marie!" Wanda held out her arms and the baby launched herself into them. "Want to go bye-bye?"

"Bye-bye! Bye-bye!" Tanya Marie bounced up and down and grabbed Wanda's hair. "Go bye-bye?"

"Yes, please," Annabelle said. "I just got to get this kitchen cleaned up. Lord knows what Laura and Jason must be thinking. I was so busy doing the wash and changing the beds I forgot all about it." Annabelle began scooping up dishes and dumping them into the sink.

"Come on, you all." Wanda shoved open the screen

door and led us outside, leaving Annabelle singing along with the radio and running hot water into the sink.

Just as we started down the back steps, a black Volkswagen painted all over with flowers pulled into the driveway.

Wanda grinned and waved. "Hey, Annabelle, guess who's here?"

"Well, I'll be!" Annabelle came down the steps faster than I would have thought possible. "Hi, Twyla. How are you, honey?"

Out of the car stepped a woman shorter than I was. Dressed in a gauzy blouse and a long batik skirt, she wore her black hair in a thick braid down to her waist and she moved across the grass with the grace of a dancer. To my surprise, the dogs didn't bark; they just lay in the shade of the house, thumping their tails lazily as Twyla walked past them.

Taking Tanya Marie from Wanda, she hugged her. "Look at you, you great big beautiful baby, how you've grown!"

Tanya Marie laughed and grabbed at one of the silver hoops dangling from Twyla's ears.

"No, no, you little imp." Twyla held the baby's hands and bounced her gently on her hip.

"What brings you out here?" Annabelle asked.

"Oh, it was just too hot in Harrisburg. I had to get away from the shop for a while, so I thought I'd drive out here and see how you all were doing."

"Well, you sure are a nice surprise, isn't she, Wanda?" Annabelle smiled.

Wanda nodded, still grinning. "This here's my friend Laura Adams and her brother Jason. They're staying down at Miss Randall's house."

Twyla smiled at me. "You must be Grace's niece. You can always tell a Randall by that red hair. Are you staying long?"

"All summer," I said, as if it were a prison sentence.

"You don't sound too happy about it." Twyla shifted the baby from one hip to the other, setting her bracelets jingling. "Are you homesick?"

I shrugged. "Sort of."

"Why don't you give the baby back to Wanda and come on inside?" Annabelle asked. "You look like you could use a nice cold glass of iced tea."

Handing Tanya Marie to Wanda, Twyla said, "Nice meeting you, Laura and Jason. Be sure and say hello to Grace for me. Tell her I'll be happy to display some of her pictures in my shop if she's got any to sell. The last batch sold fast."

She looked at me as if she were about to say something else, but she turned to Wanda instead. "Take good care of my favorite baby," she said. "Don't take her too deep into the woods."

"Don't worry." Wanda swung Tanya Marie up and down till she squealed. "See how good I treat her?"

As Wanda led us into the backyard, I thought I heard Twyla asking Annabelle about Maude. I turned around, hoping to hear more, but their voices were too low. For a second, though, Twyla's eyes met mine, and I had a feeling she was concerned about me. She actually looked worried and I thought she was going to call me back, but Annabelle took Twyla's arm and drew her up the steps into the house.

chapter

⊰8⊱

Taking a path through the woods, Wanda led us down to the creek. She plopped Tanya Marie down on the sand, then waded out into the water. I splashed in behind her.

"Will she be okay?" I looked back at Tanya Marie crawling along the sand, poking at twigs and pebbles and chuckling to herself.

"Sure, she's a real good baby, but she weighs about two tons." Wanda groaned. "She was a year old last week and I sure wish she'd start walking. She's just too fat to get her fanny off the ground."

"She's so cute." I smiled at the baby. She had pretty pink cheeks and blonde curls and two little dimples when she smiled.

"She looks just like Eddie. There's no way he could lie about being her daddy," Wanda said.

"That reminds me." I dropped my voice so Jason wouldn't hear us. "Remember what you told me about Charlene getting the love potion from Maude?"

Wanda nodded. "Yeah, but I told you it didn't do her no good."

"I'd still like to talk to her about it." I paused. Jason and Tanya Marie were laughing and a breeze was sighing in the leaves over our heads. "I want to go see Maude myself."

Wanda stared at me. "Are you crazy?"

I shook my head. "It's on account of my mother and father. I want to stop them from getting a divorce. Maude could cast a spell or something, I'm sure she could."

Wanda swung one leg back and forth in the water. "Maude can't do anything about a divorce. I told you she didn't bring Eddie back. It won't do no good to go see her, Laura."

"Well, maybe not—but do you think Charlene would tell me about her?"

"Sure, she'll tell you all about her and anything else you'd like to hear about. The problem is getting her to shut up. I've seen her keep customers talking at the Dairy Queen till their ice cream starts running down their arms."

"When does she get home?"

"Oh, round six-thirty. But you better wait till seven-thirty or eight before you come over. Charlene likes to lie down after she gets home. Says she's tired from standing on her feet all day, but I think it's working her jaws that tires her out." Wanda glanced at Tanya Marie. "Hey, get that out of your mouth!" she shouted as Tanya Marie started chewing on a stick. "Get that away from her, Jason!"

Jason looked up from his sand castle and grabbed the stick. Tanya Marie immediately burst into tears.

"Sometimes I wish I was old enough to get a job," Wanda said. "Seems to me I work harder doing nothing than Charlene does at the Dairy Queen, and she gets paid for it. It just ain't fair." Wanda waded out of the water and scooped up Tanya Marie. "Oh, what's the matter, baby?" she crooned. "Did that mean old boy take your best stick away?"

Squatting next to Jason, Wanda tried to interest Tanya Marie in building a castle. But she seemed more interested in wrecking Jason's than in building one of her own. Every time Wanda turned her back, the baby picked up a stone or a stick and put it in her mouth.

"Maybe she's hungry," Jason said, shoving her away from the tower he'd just built.

"Could be." Wanda picked up Tanya Marie. "You want to go home? See Annabelle? Have lunch?"

"Annabelle! Bye-bye! Bye-bye!" Tanya Marie bounced around on Wanda's hip, grabbing at her hair for balance.

"Maybe Twyla will still be there. You'd like to see her, wouldn't you?" Wanda asked Tanya Marie.

As the baby shifted her interest to my hair, I said, "Twyla's really beautiful, isn't she? She looks like a gypsy or a princess. Wouldn't you love to look just like her?"

Wanda snorted. "Even if I dyed my hair black, I wouldn't have a chance in this world of looking like Twyla. Would you believe she's my cousin? Once or twice removed, of course, which must be why she's so beautiful and I'm not. But you know something? As pretty as she is, she's not married or nothing. Isn't that peculiar?"

"Look at my Aunt Grace. She's not married either and she's really pretty too. Maybe neither one of them met the right man."

"Yeah, you're probably right," Wanda agreed. "Both of them are kind of strange, though, don't you think? I mean your aunt's always up at her house drawing or working in her garden and Twyla spends all her time in her little craft shop, sewing up pillows and skirts and dolls bigger than she is with weird faces made out of old nylon stockings. Seems like they both live kind of funny lives."

"Well, at least they'll never have to worry about getting divorced."

"That's true."

"Bye-bye! Bye-bye!" Tanya Marie bounced up and down and yanked hard on Wanda's hair.

"Okay, okay." Wanda gave her a big kiss. "You come on over around eight o'clock, Laura, if you want to see Charlene. Your vocal cords will get a good rest, but your ears will just shrivel up and fall off your head."

After Wanda had gone, I sat on the sand watching the creek ripple over the stones, sparkling as it flowed from sunlight into shadow and back into sunlight. Overhead a crow cawed harshly, and I jumped, startled. Just as before, the crow was perched right over my head and regarded me with yellow eyes. Reaching for a stone, I threw it as hard as I could. The crow shifted its weight on the branch, spread its wings, and slowly lifted itself into the air.

Jason and I watched it land on another limb only a few feet away. He looked at me. "I don't like that bird," he said. "It's ugly."

"I know," I picked up another stone and threw it at the crow, missing again. This time it didn't bother to change its perch. It stayed where it was, its shoulders hunched, and opened its beak wide. "Krrrrk?" it said.

"Let's go home," Jason said.

As we started up the path, a figure stepped out of the underbrush. "You children should know better than to throw stones at birds," Maude said, glaring at us. "How can a poor helpless crow possibly harm you? You should be ashamed." Standing there with her walking stick raised, she looked as if she planned to attack us.

Jason scurried behind me, burying his face in the small of my back, his arms wrapped around me. "I didn't hurt it," I said, trying to control the shaking in my voice.

"You could have put his eye out, you careless, thoughtless girl." Looking up into the branches, Maude called, "Soot, Soot, my pretty, my precious, come here and let me comfort you." The crow flapped down from the tree and settled on her shoulder, fixing its eyes on me.

As Maude crooned over the crow, I took a deep breath. "I'm sorry," I said. "I didn't know he was your pet." I hoped she'd forgive me. Otherwise I hadn't a chance of getting her to reconcile my parents.

She looked at me, her face thoughtful. "Never throw a stone at a bird again, Laura Adams," she said, her voice still angry.

I shook my head, hoping she didn't think I was the kind of person who threw stones at birds habitually. "I won't," I whispered. I felt so ashamed I could barely look at her.

Stepping closer to me, she smiled. "I'm sure you won't, Laura. Now, when are you coming to visit me? It makes me so happy to see you and think of Margaret. You would like to make an old lady happy, wouldn't you? Come sit with me and talk, tell me about yourself and your aunt and your mother, and I'll tell you about your grandmother, all the things I remember from our girlhood. It's such a pity you never knew Margaret, such a pity." Her eyes glittered as she spoke and one wrinkled hand crept up and down my arm, keeping me there close to her.

"I'll come soon," I promised, aware of Jason whimpering behind me. "We have to go home for lunch now," I added, moving away from her.

"Yes, your little brother isn't too sure of me, is he?" Maude peered around at Jason and he moved to my other side, trying to keep me between him and Maude. "Such a fine-looking little boy, so strong and healthy," she said.

"Aunt Grace is waiting for us. We really have to go." I sidled around Maude, aware that the crow was watching me. This close, it looked enormous, its beak long and sharp and deadly.

"Yes, yes, run along then, children, run along. I'll be here when you need me, Laura. Don't forget that I can help you."

"I won't. Good-bye, Miss Blackthorne." Trying to keep Jason from running, I walked away from Maude, but until the path curved sharply around a tree, I could feel her eyes following me.

chapter

⊰9⊱

"Why don't you stay here while I go over to Wanda's?" I asked Jason.

It was evening and we were sitting out on the front steps eating cherry Popsicles. Aunt Grace was lying in the rope hammock she'd hung at one end of the porch. It was warm and soft outside, calm with birdsong and sweet with the smell of cut grass. I wanted to be by myself for a while, free of Jason and his sticky little hand.

"I want to meet Charlene too." Jason stood up and wiped his hands on his shorts, obviously ready to go, bright red mouth and all.

Aunt Grace looked up from her book. "Why don't you stay here, Jason? It's almost your bedtime and you haven't had your bath yet."

"I want to go with Laurie." Jason stuck out his lower lip, a sure sign he was getting ready to cry.

"Not this evening, Jason." Aunt Grace stirred awkwardly in the hammock and got up. "Come on. I'll read you the next chapter of *The Lion, the Witch, and the Wardrobe* and then I'll pop you into the tub."

"You'll read it right now?" Jason's lower lip retreated.

"I'll go right in and get it. You and I can cuddle up in the hammock together and find out what the White Witch plans to do with Edmund."

"She's going to give him candy, isn't she?" I heard Jason say as I jumped off the porch and over the chinaberry bush. Landing on the soft grass, I sprang to my feet, turned three cartwheels and ran down the hill to the road. It was the first time I'd gone anywhere without Jason for days and I felt wonderful.

As the road dipped down into a grove of trees, I walked more slowly, thinking about Stoneleigh. At this time on a summer evening, my friends would be at the park, sitting around the fountain, talking and laughing and watching the boys cruise by on their ten-speeds. For a minute, I closed my eyes and imagined myself sitting next to Kim, laughing at one of Lisa Weinstein's jokes. I could almost hear the fountain and the shouts of kids on the playground and I wanted to go home so badly I felt like crying.

Then I thought about Maude. All I needed to do was let her help me. Why was I so afraid? I saw the park again, only this time I let Maude walk into the picture. Down one of the sandy paths she came, striding along in her rags, Soot on her shoulder, stepping around mothers pushing strollers and little kids on big wheels. Right up to the fountain she came and Lisa made a crack about her appearance. While we laughed, Maude brandished her stick at us, but she couldn't scare us. Back home in Stoneleigh no one believed in witches. At least not in broad daylight.

But it was different here in the mountains, miles

59

away from shopping centers and housing developments and superhighways. Things I would have laughed at in Stoneleigh seemed real here. In this grove of trees, already filling with shadows, Maude was more than a weird old lady to laugh at. Here she was a witch, and here I was afraid of her.

Shivering, I glanced around me at the trees crowding silently together, casting long shadows from the setting sun across the road. Afraid that Maude was near, watching me silently, I ran out of the grove and up the hill toward Wanda's house.

By the time I got there, I was hot and out of breath. Giving the yard a quick survey for dogs, I sprinted up the driveway. Wanda was sitting on the front porch railing waiting for me. "Come on up," she yelled. "Don't pay the dogs no mind. They're tied up out back."

Sitting down next to her, I took a handful of peanuts from the jar she handed me. Inside the living room, I could see the back of Annabelle's head. She was watching a game show on television. "Mississippi!" she yelled at a contestant. "Mississippi, you dummy!"

Wanda rolled her eyes. "She just loves watching those greedy fools jumping up and down like idiots cause they won a refrigerator or something."

Just then the screen door opened and a girl stepped out onto the porch. She had long blonde hair and eyes as big and blue as Tanya Marie's. Although she didn't look old enough to be anybody's mother, I knew she must be Charlene.

"You must be Laura," she said. When she smiled she had dimples like Tanya Marie's and a gap between her teeth like Wanda's. "I'm Charlene." She flipped her hair out of her eyes and sat down beside me. Taking a pack of cigarettes out of her back pocket, she lit one and exhaled a cloud of smoke. "Want one?" she asked me.

I shook my head, amazed. Nobody in my whole life had ever offered me a cigarette. "I don't smoke," I said, feeling very unsophisticated.

"Give me one." Wanda reached for the cigarettes, but Charlene put the pack back in her pocket.

"You're already too little and skinny and short, you know that. You want to grow up to be a midget or something?"

"Aw, come on, Charlene. You were going to give Laura one." Wanda tried to grab the cigarette Charlene was smoking.

"I said no, Wanda Louise, and I meant it!" Charlene slapped Wanda's hand. "Laura's company. And she's tall enough so it won't hurt her none." Charlene gestured at the back of Annabelle's head. "And you know what she'd do if she saw you with a cigarette in your mouth!" Charlene exhaled a pale cloud of smoke and watched it linger for a second in the air.

"Wanda says you're from Washington, D.C. Is that right?" Charlene looked at me.

I nodded. "Actually we live in the suburbs, sort of out in the country, not too far from Gaithersburg."

"Gaithersburg? Never heard of it. I wouldn't mind living in Washington, though, working for the government or something. A couple of my girlfriends got jobs there last summer. They have a little apartment somewhere and they just love it. I bet you find this a real dull place, just nothing to do at all."

"It's nice here," I said, not wanting to hurt Wanda's feelings. "It's different though. We don't have anybody like Maude where I live."

Charlene laughed. "You really want to hear about that old crackpot? I tell you the truth, honey, she didn't do a thing for me. It's been over half a year since she sold me that love potion and I ain't seen Eddie yet."

"Well, what happened? What was it like to go see her? Was it scary?" I stared at Charlene, wanting to hear every detail. The pink sky behind her turned the ends of her hair gold and she looked like a movie star sitting there enjoying all the attention I was giving her.

"Well, one day when Tanya Marie was about six months old, I was in Blue Hollow doing some errands. I was really feeling down, you know? Seeing all these places Eddie and me used to go, looking at all kinds of couples, teenagers and adults and everybody. Seemed like everybody had somebody but me. All I had was this cute little baby and a dumb job in the Dairy Queen. I mean, what kind of a life is that?" Charlene flicked her cigarette butt out across the yard and watched it burn itself out in the grass.

"Then I saw Maude, hobbling along with that crow on her shoulder, mumbling to herself like a crazy woman, and the thought came to me that maybe she could help me. I'd heard lots of talk about her doing stuff for people romantically, so I decided to ask her."

Charlene flipped her hair back and looked at me. "Now, Laura, I have never been a brave person and all my life I been scared to death of that old woman, but I was so desperate to get Eddie back that I walked right up to her and asked if she could help me. Well, she just stood there staring at me, she and that bird both, and my knees felt like they were turning to water. I thought I was going to faint dead away in the street when she reaches out and grabs my wrist like this."

Charlene grabbed my wrist so hard she scared me to death. I almost fell right off the railing.

"Then she says, 'What do you need? A love potion?' Just like she could read my mind, I swear."

Even though it was warm there on the porch, I shivered.

" 'Yes,' I says in this squeaky little voice," Charlene continued. " 'Come see me tonight, my dear, I'll give you what you need,' Maude said. And she laughed just like a witch in a fairy tale, I swear she did." Charlene raised her right hand.

"Then she walked away and that night I went to see her and I was so scared going through those dark woods I thought I'd die before I got there. I was shaking and crying and cussing Eddie 'cause it was all his fault I was out there all by myself where anybody could grab me and knock me on the side of the head or something. And it was even worse when I got to Maude's place. She was waiting for me and there wasn't a light anywhere. Just the moon shining down through the trees. She lit one candle and took me inside." Charlene took out another cigarette and busied herself lighting it.

"Everytime you tell this story it's different," Wanda said. "You just keep adding and adding till I get so bored I could fall asleep sitting here." Wanda yawned widely.

"You want to take flying lessons, Wanda Louise? You want to see how far I can throw you?" Charlene glared across me at Wanda.

"You just never said nothing bout her lighting one candle before, Charlene. That's new." Wanda slid down the railing, putting a little distance between herself and Charlene.

"What happened next?" I whispered, giving Wanda a look that meant for her to be quiet.

"Well, it was dark in her house, even with the candle. I could hardly see my hand before my face. And it smelled funny too. Not bad exactly, just strange, like maybe she was burning herbs or something. She sat me down near the fire and she asked me all these questions about Eddie and she kept staring at me all the time. The crow was sitting up on the mantelpiece and he was staring at me, too. I was so scared I could hardly talk."

"Hmmmph!" Wanda snorted. "Wish I could hire Maude to keep you scared."

Charlene rolled her eyes and ignored Wanda. "She took all these herbs and things and mixed them together and she chanted a lot of mumbo jumbo and wrote things down on paper and burned things. I never saw anything like it. I mean she just carried on, worse than a preacher at a revival."

"And then what?"

Charlene shook her head. "She charged me ten dollars and I left and that was six months ago and I ain't seen Eddie yet." Charlene sighed and tossed the second cigarette butt after the first one. "I guess she's just a crazy old lady like everybody says. She ain't no more a witch than you or me or Wanda. She just knows how to put on a good show."

The light from the sunset had dwindled to a narrow band of pink sky just above the mountains, but even in the twilight I could see the disappointment in Charlene's face. "There's still time for it to work," I said. "Maybe Eddie's too far away for the spell to reach him."

Charlene shrugged. "I used to tell myself that, but

six months, shoot. That's a long time, honey." She gazed past Wanda and me at the mountains. "It sure would be nice if he came back, though, it really would. I get so tired of slaving away at the Dairy Queen. If Eddie came back we could go away to someplace like California or Hawaii where it's always sunny and I'd never have to see a Dairy Queen again."

"They got Dairy Queens in California and Hawaii, Charlene. I hate to tell you, but they got Dairy Queens all over the world," Wanda said.

"Well, I wouldn't be working in one, Wanda. I could just look the other way and keep on going whenever I saw one."

"Hey, Charlene," Annabelle called from the living room, dark now except for the television's blue glow. "What are you telling those girls?" Then Annabelle appeared in the doorway.

"Oh, nothing. They just wanted to hear about Maude and that dumb love potion." Charlene yawned and stretched, seeming bored with the whole subject.

Annabelle looked at us. "What do you want to know about Maude for? She hasn't been bothering you, has she?"

"Course not," Wanda said. "She couldn't bother me if she tried."

Annabelle turned to me. "You sure she hasn't pestered you none?"

I shook my head. "She's talked to me a few times. She told me about my grandmother and her, how they were friends and all." I tried to picture Maude and my grandmother as young women, girls like Wanda and me, but I'd never seen my grandmother and I couldn't imagine someone as old as Maude ever being young.

65

Annabelle frowned. "I've heard they were friends once." Shifting her weight from one hip to the other, she stared at me as if she wanted to tell me something but didn't have the words for it. "You stay away from her, both of you. I don't want either one of you going near that old woman. You hear?"

We nodded to show we heard her, but I knew I had no intention of staying away from Maude. I needed her too badly. After all, what did I have to lose? Even if she couldn't help me, she couldn't make my life any worse than it already was.

"What are you trying to do, Annabelle? Scare the poor kids to death?" Charlene brushed her hair back from her forehead. "You know that old woman's a fake. All she done for me was make me ten dollars poorer."

"Talk to Twyla about Maude someday," Annabelle said. "She'll tell you an earful." Annabelle frowned at Charlene. "You ain't as smart as you think you are, girl. There's lots you don't know about."

Charlene shrugged. "Twyla don't know everything either. She's just as phony as Maude, if you ask me. Sweeping around like some kind of princess in her long skirts, running that dumb little shop with all those expensive things, telling fortunes like a carnival gypsy. You wait, by the time she's Maude's age, Twyla'll be walking around with a crow on her shoulder, talking to herself and casting spells."

Charlene jumped down from the railing, causing it to sway, and tossed her cigarette out into the darkness. "You all want to watch a movie with Annabelle and me? It's the one where this girl gets possessed by the devil and does all these weird things. Her head turns around backwards and she throws up green slime and she floats over the bed. You all want to come in and watch it?"

"I already saw it," Wanda said. "It was all fake. You could tell the fake stuff without half looking."

"You were scared to death and you know it, Wanda Louise Orton. You wouldn't go to sleep without a light on for at least two weeks after you saw it."

"Bull." Wanda hopped down from the railing, glaring at Charlene as if she were about to attack her.

Charlene snorted, swung her hair out of her face and opened the screen door. "Nice meeting you, Laura. Come on over sometime and I'll do your hair. I just love fooling around with hairstyles. I'm thinking of going to beauty school if I can ever save up enough money."

Annabelle lingered by the door, still staring at Wanda and me. "I'm not fooling about Maude. She's a mean old woman, full of spite, and she don't care who she hurts." She looked hard at me, but I just looked down at my feet. I didn't like the worry I saw on Annabelle's face.

"I'm walking Laura part way home, okay?" Wanda slid off the railing and I hopped off too.

"Be careful. That road's got some dark places," Annabelle said.

Charlene looked out the window at us. "Bye, Laura. Wanda, you be sure and run all the way home, so nothing'll grab you in the dark. Course they'd let you go as soon as it got light, but don't take no chances."

Wanda made a face at Charlene, but she'd already turned her attention to the television screen. "Come on." Wanda ran down the steps and I followed her.

The night air was cool and sweet with the smell of

67

honeysuckle, and the sky was dusted all over with stars, more stars than I could ever remember seeing at Stoneleigh. Standing still for a moment, I tipped my head back, staring up at the sky, finding the Big Dipper, the Milky Way, and what I thought might be Orion.

"Come on, Laura." Wanda stood in the middle of the road, her shadow black against the moon-washed dirt. "Quit poking along like a snail."

"It's a beautiful night, isn't it?" I walked slowly, listening to the crickets chirping in the field and a mockingbird singing in the woods somewhere.

Wanda nodded, looking uneasily at the grove of trees lying in shadow at the foot of the hill. "What do you think Annabelle was trying to do?"

I shrugged. "You mean all that stuff about Maude? Maybe she just doesn't like her." I looked at Wanda, wondering if Annabelle had scared her as much as she'd scared me. Not that I planned to admit it. I was sure that if I told Wanda how afraid I was, she'd never go near Maude.

"Suppose she's right, though?"

"I don't care what Annabelle says. Or Charlene either. I'm going to ask Maude to make my parents stay married." I frowned at Wanda. "And if you won't come with me, I'll go by myself."

"I think I better get on back home. It's late," Wanda said.

"But we're not even halfway to Aunt Grace's house. Aren't you at least going to walk me through the woods?" I stared at her, feeling betrayed.

Wanda shook her head. "If I walk through the woods with you, then I got to walk back by myself."

"How about halfway through the woods? Will you walk that far?" I pleaded, aware that my voice was rising to a Jason-like whine.

But Wanda was already inching backwards up the road. "Just run," she said. "Just run as fast as you can toward your house and I'll run toward mine."

"Please come with me, just a little way?" The more we talked, the darker those woods got.

"I'll come to your house tomorrow, okay?" Wanda called from the top of the hill.

"Don't bother!" I shouted. "If you can't come with me now, don't come tomorrow either! Don't come ever!"

Taking a deep breath, I turned and ran toward home, wincing when my bare feet struck against loose stones. As I plunged into the darkness under the trees, I saw something move in the shadows at the side of the road. Before I could dodge aside, Maude stepped into my path, blocking my way.

"Well, well, Laura Adams, where are you going in such a hurry in the dark? You almost knocked me down, child." Maude smiled at me, but the hand that grasped my arm was cold and strong.

"I'm sorry, I didn't see you," I stammered, my lips stiff.

"Well, now, I saw you coming, Laura Adams, and I heard you too, but then these old eyes and ears of mine are sharp as a cat's. They work better in the dark than they do in the daylight." Maude peered at me, her eyes searching my face. "Now I've gone and frightened you, haven't I?"

Turning her eyes to Soot, who was riding her shoulder like a small demon of the night, she said, "We are

69

a frightening pair, aren't we? The two of us roaming the woods day and night, as we have for years, shunning the company of other human beings. But we mean no harm to this child, do we?" Maude chuckled and stared at me, her eyes glittering in the moonlight.

"My aunt is expecting me home. She'll be worrying," I whispered, backing away from Maude.

"Ah, now, I wouldn't want to worry your aunt." She reached out and stroked my hair back from my face. "Such a pretty girl," she crooned, "such a pretty, pretty girl. How proud Margaret would have been of you, Laura."

I stood still, letting her stroke my hair, afraid to move, afraid to ask her to help me.

"Charlene told you all about me, didn't she?" Maude asked softly. "You'd like to ask me to use my power to help you, too, wouldn't you? You needn't be afraid of me, Laura." Maude smiled at me as she bent nearer, her voice soft and low.

"How do you know I need any help?" I whispered.

"I have ways of knowing things, my dear. I have the power to know and help."

"But Eddie hasn't come back to Charlene, he didn't marry her, you didn't help her." I tried again to back away from her, but her grip on my arm was tight.

"He hasn't yet, Laura, but he will, he will. Everything comes in time, everything." Maude continued to stroke my hair, harder and harder, her fingers raking through it like a comb.

"You're hurting me," I whispered, tears stinging my eyes. It felt as if she were actually yanking hairs from my head.

Maude's face softened. "I'm sorry. I didn't mean to

hurt you. Your hair was tangled and I wanted to smooth it, that's all." She smiled, splitting her face into millions of crisscrossing wrinkles. "Now, shall I help you? Will you let me?"

"Could you really stop the divorce?" I asked.

Maude nodded and gestured up at the sky, hidden by the dense leaves of the trees. "Yes, I can stop it. Come to me tomorrow night, Laura, if you want my help." She smiled again and Soot shifted restlessly, his strong taloned feet digging into Maude's shoulder. "But don't tell your aunt. Grace Randall doesn't believe in witchcraft. She'd never allow you to seek my help. It must be our secret, Laura, ours alone."

I stared into her eyes, still afraid of her, not sure whether I should trust her or not.

"You will need to bring a few things with you if I'm to help you," Maude said softly. "You must bring something that belongs to your parents; a picture of the two of them together will do. I will also need something that belongs to Jason and something of Grace's too. One of her brushes would do nicely. To make a binding spell I must have things from the whole family."

"Should I bring something of mine?"

"Yours?" Maude chuckled. "No, no. Just being there will be enough for you, my dear child."

"How much will it cost? I've got thirty dollars left from my summer spending money."

"No, no, Laura. I've known your family for a long time, a very long time. Let's say I'm doing this in memory of my friendship with Margaret." She smiled into the darkness behind me and Soot stirred again, ruffling his wings. "Now go on home, Laura dear. I shall expect

71

you tomorrow night. If you're frightened of walking through the woods in the dark, you may bring Wanda with you, but no one else is to know, not even Annabelle." Maude stepped off the road onto a narrow path I hadn't noticed before and waved her stick at me. "Good night, my dear. I shall look forward to your visit tomorrow night."

As the shadows closed around Maude, I ran up the road toward home, my heart pounding with fear.

chapter

⊰ 10 ⊱

When I got home, Aunt Grace was sitting on the front steps waiting for me.

"Where have you been Laura? I expected you back over an hour ago." She smiled at me. "I was afraid something had snatched you away."

I stood at the bottom of the steps, looking up at her, feeling uncomfortable about the promise I'd made to Maude. "I'm sorry. I forgot all about the time. We were watching TV and talking and stuff, you know." I edged up the steps, wanting to get past her and into the house, then upstairs to the privacy of my room.

Aunt Grace patted the step next to her. "Why don't you sit down and join me for a while? It's such a lovely night. Just smell the honeysuckle, Laura, and look at all those stars." Aunt Grace hugged her knees, her face soft and young in the moonlight.

"I was thinking of going up to bed," I said hesitantly. "I'm kind of tired tonight. But I guess I could sit for a little while." Uneasily I dropped down on the step next to her, wishing I could just run upstairs and pull the covers over my head.

"Did you run all the way home? You're out of breath." Aunt Grace smoothed my hair, and I flinched, remembering the touch of Maude's bony hand. "You weren't scared, were you?"

I shook my head and we sat quietly for a while, listening to the crickets and gazing across the valley at the mountains, silvery and unreal in the moonlight.

"How's Annabelle?" Aunt Grace asked.

"Oh, she's okay. She and Charlene were getting set to watch a horror film."

"I hate scary movies," Aunt Grace said.

"Some of them aren't so bad. And most of them are too dumb to be scary."

"Real life is scary enough for me."

I stared at her, surprised. "What are you scared of?"

Aunt Grace smiled. "I've got my share of little fears hidden away, Laura. Everybody does."

I knew I did and I knew Jason did. He never even tried to hide his. And Wanda was scared of the dark and Maude and horror movies and who knew what else? But it was hard to imagine Aunt Grace afraid. Unlike Mom, she seemed brave, ready to face anything.

"I thought Mom was the coward of the family," I said, "not you. She was nervous every single night here. She kept locking the doors and closing the curtains and turning on lights. You never even bother with stuff like that."

Aunt Grace got up and I followed her into the house. "Your Mom got married and she had you and Jason," she said as I paused at the foot of the stairs. "That's something."

I stared at her, puzzled. "What's brave about that? The way it turned out, it was just plain stupid, not brave."

74

Kissing my cheek, Aunt Grace sent me upstairs. "It's more than I ever did," she said softly.

I looked back at her, but she had already turned away. I stood still for a moment, listening to her footsteps, and then I went upstairs quietly, taking care not to wake Jason.

As soon as I was in bed, I curled up into a tight ball under the covers and tried not to think about Maude and my promise to visit her. I was glad she'd said I could bring Wanda with me, but I wasn't sure Wanda would come. She hadn't shown much courage walking me home and it was hard to imagine her actually going to Maude's house.

I fell asleep worrying about Wanda and when I woke up the sun was shining in my eyes, a sure sign that it was after ten o'clock already. As usual, I could hear Jason chattering away in the kitchen, and I smiled, thinking how happy he would be when Mom and Dad came to get us.

Looking at the dresser, I saw the picture I needed. I'd taken it last summer at Ocean City with the little Instamatic camera Daddy had given me for my tenth birthday. In it, Mom and Dad, dressed in bathing suits, smiled at me, a little out of focus, the sun in their eyes, but looking as happy as anyone on a vacation should look. If the truth were known, they'd been quarreling about something before I'd gotten out my camera, but they'd smiled for the picture. Dad had even put his arm around Mom, making them look like a honeymoon couple instead of the parents of two kids, one of whom was pouting in the background, his back turned, his head bent over his sand bucket.

After I got dressed, I went into Jason's room. Although he hadn't been here very long, he'd already duplicated his room at home. Clothes on the floor, toys and books scattered everywhere, Lego pieces cleverly strewn about in places most likely to injure your bare feet, the bed as rumpled as if an elephant had slept in it.

Selecting a Matchbox car from one of many parked in and around a Lego garage, I went back to my room and hid it in my underwear drawer, next to the photograph of Mom and Dad. Now all I needed was one of Aunt Grace's brushes.

Downstairs, Aunt Grace and Jason were washing the dishes. "Laura," Aunt Grace asked, "do you want to go into Blue Hollow with Jason and me? I have to do some grocery shopping."

"No, not today." I sat down at the table to drink a glass of orange jurice. "I promised Wanda I'd come over and help her with Tanya Marie."

"Is that Charlene's baby?" Aunt Grace asked.

I nodded. "She's really cute, but she's kind of a pain. Wanda gets stuck with her all the time, which doesn't seem too fair to me."

"Poor Charlene doesn't have much choice. She has to work. Annabelle's got some kind of a pension, but I don't think it amounts to much."

"When Charlene and Eddie get married, things'll be a lot better," I said.

"Is Charlene getting married? I thought the baby's father disappeared." Aunt Grace stared at me, surprised.

"Maude's bringing him back," Jason said.

"Maude?" Aunt Grace said. "Did Charlene go to Maude? I thought she had more sense than that."

"That's what Wanda told us," I said, thinking fast. Taking my glass to the sink, I gave Jason a quick pinch on the arm to remind him to keep his mouth shut. "She says lots of people go to Maude for help with stuff like that."

Aunt Grace shook her head. "I had no idea people still believed in that nonsense. What's the matter, Jason?"

Jason was rubbing his arm and whimpering. "Nothing," he whined, edging away from me.

"Well, you have a nice time at Wanda's, Laura. We'll be back sometime after lunch." After gathering her purse and her car keys, Aunt Grace herded Jason out the door.

As soon as I heard the station wagon pull away from the house, I darted across the room to Aunt Grace's drawing table. Barely glancing at the unfinished painting of a fern lying there, I grabbed a small brush from an earthenware jar and took it upstairs. I shoved it into the drawer with the photograph and the Matchbox car, then went back downstairs.

I ran all the way to the grove of trees where I'd seen Maude last night. Then I stopped, almost afraid to go on. Suppose she was hiding there in the shade, waiting for me? Squinting ahead, I saw no one on the road. A mourning dove called sadly from the green shade, a gentle breeze ruffled the leaves, and sunlight instead of moonlight dappled the road. Of course, she could be on the path or behind a tree and Soot could be anywhere, his yellow eyes watching me. But there was no sound, no sign of either one of them, just the trees and the mourning dove and the sun.

Telling myself I had nothing to fear from Maude, that she wanted to help me out of kindness, that she wasn't about to ask me for my soul or anything like that, I ran through the grove without looking to the right or the left. Out again in the sunlight, I slowed to a walk, trying to get my breath back before I got to Wanda's.

As soon as I was in sight of the house, the dogs set up their usual chorus of barks and growls. I figured it was safe, though, because I could see Wanda sitting on the front porch, bouncing Tanya Marie on her lap. When she saw me, she shouted at the dogs and, with the baby on her hip, staggered down the hill to meet me. Even at a distance I could tell she was excited about something.

"Guess who's here?" She pointed at a small blue pickup truck parked in front of the house.

"How should I know?" If Wanda couldn't even apologize for not walking me home last night, why should I care who was visiting her?

"Eddie's here. That's his brand-new truck."

"Car go! Car go!" Tanya Marie cried, bouncing harder on Wanda's hip.

"He drove up to the Dairy Queen this morning and he and Charlene had a long talk," Wanda said. "Then Charlene's boss started yelling at her for talking to the customers, and Eddie told him to shut up. Then her boss fired her and right now she's inside packing her stuff. They're going off together, all three of them." Wanda hugged Tanya Marie. "Oh, I'm going to miss you!" She gave the baby a big slobbery kiss and Tanya Marie laughed and made a face.

"Miss you! Miss you!" Tanya Marie crowed.

"He came back just like that?" I stared at Wanda, forgetting to be mad.

Wanda nodded. "Charlene said she like to have fainted when she looked up and saw him standing there, all squinty-eyed in the sun."

"Do you think Maude's spell worked after all?" I felt kind of watery-kneed just thinking about it.

Wanda shrugged. "Don't know," she said. "Might have though."

"I saw her in the grove last night, Wanda," I said. "After you ran off and left me there all by myself."

Wanda's eyes widened and she gripped Tanya Marie tighter. "What did she do?"

"She could've killed me for all you knew." I stared coldly at Wanda. "But she didn't. She said she could stop my parents from getting a divorce. She also said that Eddie would come back to Charlene. She said all things come in time."

Wanda shook her head and looked around uneasily. Shifting Tanya Marie to her other hip, she said, "Just look at my arms. All the hairs are sticking straight up. I got goose bumps all over."

"She wants me to come to her house tonight, Wanda. Will you come with me? She said you could."

"Me? I wouldn't go near that old woman's house for nothing! Are you crazy?"

"Please, Wanda. Just think what she's done for Charlene. If she were really horrible, she wouldn't have helped her. If you help people with love, you must be a good witch, don't you think?"

Wanda jiggled Tanya Marie. "I don't know." She shook her head. "I just don't know, Laura. I always been scared of her, all my life." She thrust Tanya Marie at me. "Here. You hold this ton of bricks for a while. She's wearing me out."

"Ton of bricks, ton of bricks," Tanya Marie said and grabbed a handful of my hair.

"Wanda?" Charlene called from the front porch.

"Bring Tanya Marie up here. I got to get her dressed."

Just as I handed Tanya Marie to Charlene, Eddie shoved the screen door open and stepped outside. Although he wasn't as handsome as I'd hoped he'd be, he was kind of good-looking in a tough way. He wore his hair shoulder-length and sort of shaggy, and he had a scraggly little mustache and beard. His eyes were close-set and small and both his nose and his teeth were crooked. Although he was wearing high-heeled cowboy boots, he wasn't quite as tall as Charlene, maybe because her sandals had very high heels.

"This here is Laura, Wanda's friend," Charlene said.

I smiled and said "hi," but Eddie barely looked at me. I might have been a little bug or something as far as he was concerned.

Without saying anything to either Wanda or me, Eddie sat down on the railing and took a swallow out of a can of beer. He didn't even look when the screen door slammed behind Charlene. Reaching into his back pocket, he took out a pack of cigarettes and lit one.

Wanda sidled up to him, smiled, and said, "Can I have one, Eddie?"

"Hell, no." Eddie gazed off at the mountains and drank some more beer, tipping his head back so that his Adam's apple stuck out and bobbed up and down.

"Aw, come on, Eddie. Charlene lets me," Wanda persisted.

"I said no." Eddie frowned at Wanda. "You ask me one more time, girl, and you won't be eating for a while."

"How come?" Wanda stared at him.

" 'Cause I'll knock every one of them pearly little teeth down your throat. Now go play dolls or something and leave me be." He laughed as if he was just teasing her, but I wasn't so sure it was all a joke. His eyes were sort of mean looking.

To my relief, Wanda opened the screen door and started to go inside. "I sure don't play with no dolls!" she said from the doorway, but Eddie was staring off into space as if she didn't exist any more. "Stupid!" she muttered. "Keep your old cigarettes all to yourself and die of lung cancer. See if I care."

If Eddie heard her, he didn't have anything to say, so we went inside.

Annabelle was sitting in front of the television set staring glumly at two people trying to win a trip to Las Vegas. "Fireman!" she shouted. "Football player! Motorcycle cop! Soldier!"

From down the hall, I could hear Tanya Marie fussing. "Hold still!" Charlene shouted. "Don't you want your daddy to be proud of you?"

"Oh, Lord," Annabelle sighed. "Oh, Lord." She swallowed some coffee and added, "I told you to say fireman!" The fat woman on television was crying because she'd just lost the trip to Las Vegas and the quizmaster was trying to cheer her up by telling her she was going to receive a lifetime's supply of dishwasher detergent.

"Where do they get these people?" Annabelle waved at the TV screen. "I swear they find the dumbest people in the whole U. S. of A. to be on this show. Charlene could get on it easy, her and Eddie both."

Ignoring Annabelle, Wanda led me down the hall to Charlene's room. Charlene was sitting on the bed with Tanya Marie in her lap, trying to pull a dress over the struggling baby's head.

"No, no! No dress!" Tanya Marie screamed.

"Sit still, dammit! Don't you ever say no to me!" Charlene shouted, her face red with anger. Then she hit Tanya Marie, slapped her so hard it made a sound like someone cracking a whip.

"Don't you ever hit that baby again!" Annabelle entered the room and snatched the screaming baby out of Charlene's arms and tried to comfort her.

"I didn't mean to hit her!" Charlene cried, tears running down her cheeks. "I just got to get her ready. Suppose Eddie gets tired of waiting and runs off again?"

"It'd be no big loss," Annabelle said, rocking Tanya Marie on her hip.

"What the hell's going on in here?" Eddie stuck his head through the doorway. "What's wrong with the kid?"

"Nothing." Charlene tossed her hair back and smiled at Eddie. "She just didn't want to get her dress on."

"You ready?" Eddie looked around the little room, taking in the dolls and stuffed animals heaped in the middle of the bed, the suitcase bulging with Charlene's clothes, the cardboard cartons full of Tanya Marie's toys, the dresses, skirts, and coats draped over a chair. "You ain't taking all this, are you?"

"It'll fit in the truck, won't it?" Charlene smiled at him.

"I doubt it. And I told you all I got is a one-bedroom apartment in Wheeling. I sure ain't got room for all this junk." He picked up a long-haired doll wearing a red satin dress and tossed it to Wanda. "Give all this stuff to your sister," he said to Charlene.

"I told you I don't play with dolls!" Wanda threw the doll back on the bed and glared at Eddie, but he picked up a box of Tanya Marie's things and walked out of the room.

"Just leave all this stuff for now, Charlene. You can always get it later." Annabelle slipped a dress over Tanya Marie's head and smoothed her curls. "Now don't you look just beautiful?"

Annabelle hugged Tanya Marie. "If things don't work out, Charlene, you can always come back here."

"Things are going to be just fine." Charlene looked at herself in her dresser mirror and fluffed her hair. "He just has to get used to the idea of marriage, that's all. He'll make a fine husband for me and a wonderful daddy for Tanya Marie. I just know he will."

"I hope so." Annabelle left the room, crooning to Tanya Marie.

Charlene bent down to pick up her suitcase, but changed her mind and hugged Wanda instead. "See? Things are working out just fine after all. Didn't I always say they would?" Waving an arm at the pile of dolls and animals, she added, "You really can have them all, Wanda. You take good care of them, though. I don't want to find them all messed up when I come visiting."

Wanda looked embarrassed. "Don't worry, Charlene. They'll be okay."

"Well, you take care of yourself, Wanda. I'll write and tell you all about married life." Charlene laughed, "Well, maybe not all. You're kind of young yet." Charlene kissed Wanda on both cheeks and picked up her suitcase. "Here, help me carry some of this stuff, will you?"

Picking up a box, we followed Charlene outside. When the truck was loaded, Charlene kissed everybody goodbye, even me, and climbed in beside Eddie. Holding Tanya Marie on her lap, she waved and blew kisses, and Eddie nodded glumly at us all. With a grating

83

sound, he shifted into first gear and drove down the driveway.

Charlene leaned out the window, her hair blowing around her face, and waved again. "Bye-bye, you all! Bye-bye!" she shouted.

Then the truck turned out onto the road and disappeared around a curve, leaving a cloud of dust behind.

Annabelle stared after the truck, shaking her head. "Oh, well," she said to nobody in particular, "I guess I'll go on up to the house and watch some TV."

We stood there in the hot sun, watching Annabelle climb the sagging steps. The door slammed shut behind her and then there was silence.

"Let's go on down to the creek. It's cooler there," Wanda said.

We cut through the woods behind Wanda's house and waded into the water, splashing each other till we were soaked and a little cooler.

"Annabelle didn't seem very happy about Charlene and Eddie," I said after a while. I was kind of puzzled about the whole thing myself. Eddie certainly hadn't acted especially happy about being there; in fact, he'd been downright unpleasant, surly, and unfriendly—not the least bit romantic. I was very disappointed in him and I had a feeling that Charlene was disappointed too. I couldn't believe that she really thought Eddie was going to be a good husband or a wonderful daddy. He just didn't show any signs of it at all.

Wanda skipped a stone across the creek. "Five times." She looked pleased. "I never skipped one more than four times before." She bent down to look for another stone. "Annabelle don't think much of Eddie," she said. "Never has. She was always trying to run him off before he got Charlene pregnant. They used to have some really awful scenes, her and Charlene, about Eddie."

"Does Eddie always act so mean and grumpy?"

Wanda nodded. "I never seen him smile or act nice to nobody. I think Charlene's crazy to go off with him." Wanda sighed and skipped another stone across the water. "Just three this time. Guess that makes it about average."

I waded farther out in the creek, feeling the cool water creep up around my knees. "Poor Tanya Marie," I said, more to myself than to Wanda.

"What do you mean?" Wanda skipped another stone across the water, frowning as it sank after only two hops.

"Well, if Charlene comes back to Annabelle instead of getting married, Tanya Marie won't have a father after all. I kind of wanted her to have a family."

"There's worse things than not having a father." Wanda kicked a spray of water in my direction. "And she'll have a family with Charlene and Annabelle and me, just like she's always had."

"You can't have a family without a father."

"Are you kidding?" Wanda stared at me as if I'd lost my mind. "I never had a father I can remember, but I've had a family all my life. My brothers and my sister and Annabelle. I never even had a mother, but I sure had a family!"

"Maybe it's because you don't remember your father. But as far as I'm concerned, our family ended the day my dad left." I looked at Wanda curiously. "Don't you ever wish your mother and father would come back?"

Wanda shook her head. "When I was little I used to, but I hardly ever think about them now. If they were to walk in the front door one day and say they were here to take me away to a new home, I wouldn't go. I'd stay right here with Annabelle."

I looked past Wanda, at the sunlight making shiny patches on the water. "I want my mother and father to live together, and I won't feel like a family until they do." I paused and looked at Wanda. "That's why it's so important for me to go to Maude's tonight. Will you come with me, Wanda? Please?"

Now it was Wanda's turn to look away, to bend over the water and look for stones to skip. Finally she stood up straight and smiled kind of unsurely at me. "If you really want me to, I will, but I wish you wouldn't go there at all. I wish you'd just leave things alone."

I grinned at her, relieved that I wouldn't have to go by myself. "Do you think Annabelle would let you spend the night at my house? I know Aunt Grace wouldn't mind."

"Sure she would."

"Go on home and ask her, okay? If she says no, we'll think of something else. But don't tell her about Maude. She might not let you come if she knew we were going to her house."

"If it's okay with Annabelle, I'll come over after supper." Wanda climbed up the bank. At the top, she stopped and looked down at me. "I sure hope we aren't going to be sorry about doing this."

"Why would we be sorry? Having my mother and father together again would be the best thing in the whole world."

Wanda didn't smile. She just stood there, staring at me. "What about Charlene and Eddie? Maybe the kind of spells Maude casts don't bring happiness, Laura."

"That's ridiculous, Wanda. Maude was my grandmother's friend. She wants to help me, I know she does."

Wanda shrugged. "I hope so, Laura." She edged away from me, turned, and ran up the path into the woods. "I'll see you later," she called, and crashed off through the bushes.

As the woods slowly grew quiet, I waded ashore, thinking about what Wanda had said. Suppose she were right? I shook my head. No, that was crazy. Not only was Maude my grandmother's friend, but my mother and father weren't like Charlene and Eddie. They were older and smarter and deep down inside they really loved each other. All they needed was a push in the right direction, and Maude was just the person to give it to them.

"Krrrrk?"

Startled, I looked up. There was a crow perched on a branch, staring down at me.

"Well, well, Laura Adams, our paths cross again." Maude stood in the path, as still as a statue, leaning upon her stick and smiling at me. "My, my, did I scare you again? My step is quiet, isn't it?"

When I didn't say anything, she smiled even more and stepped closer to me. "Am I to expect you tonight? You know now that my spells work, do you not? As I granted Charlene's wish, I can grant yours, Laura. I can give you a family. A mother and a father, a son and a daughter, the way it should be."

"Yes." I stared at Maude, her layers of skirts, dresses, petticoats, shawls, sweaters and scarves fluttering about her, soiled and frayed. "Yes, I'll come." My heart pounded so hard against my ribs I was sure Maude could hear it.

"And Wanda will come with you." Maude nodded,

87

chuckling to herself, her hands twisting her walking stick. "Tonight at midnight, Laura Adams, in memory of Margaret Randall. I'll be waiting."

Without saying more, Maude turned and made her way back into the woods, her progress slow but barely audible. No swishing branches, no rustlings underfoot. One minute she was there, Soot on her shoulder, and the next she was gone, fading into the greenery as silently as a dream.

chapter

~11~

From eight o'clock on, I sat out on the front steps waiting for Wanda. The sun was almost level with the mountaintops, sending long shadows across the lawn, and a small crescent moon, no bigger than a thumbnail clipping, was already floating in the pale blue sky.

"When's Wanda coming anyway?" Jason was sitting next to me, trying to finish his Popsicle before it melted and ran down his arm in a sticky orange trickle.

I pointed down the road. Wanda was coming around the curve below the house. The setting sun touched her hair with fire and her shadow stretched so long it looked as if it were cast by someone walking on stilts.

Leaving Jason behind, I vaulted off the porch and ran to meet her. "Where have you been? It's almost nine o'clock!"

Wanda laughed. "Mr. Evans came over to keep Annabelle company, and he had to show me all his little tricks, like pulling quarters out of my ears and stuff like that. He does the same ones every time, and if he let me keep all those quarters, I'd be rich by now!"

"Who's Mr. Evans?"

"Annabelle's boyfriend."

I laughed. "Annabelle's boyfriend? How could Annabelle have a boyfriend? She must be almost sixty years old!"

"That don't make no difference."

"But she's even older than Aunt Grace!"

Wanda looked puzzled. "Don't your aunt have a boyfriend?"

"Are you kidding?" I burst out laughing again, trying to imagine Aunt Grace having a date.

"How about your mother and father? I bet they have plenty of dates."

"They do not!" Suddenly it wasn't funny. I glared at Wanda, furious with her for suggesting such a thing about my parents. If I hadn't needed her to go with me to Maude's, I'd have really told her off, but I bit my tongue and didn't say anything else.

"Well, Annabelle's had boyfriends as long as I can remember. She says life ain't worth living without a man." Wanda giggled.

"That's dumb for someone her age to talk like that."

Wanda shrugged. "That's what she says. She goes to this place sometimes in Harrisburg called the Adam and Eve Club. It's one of those singles bars, you know, where people like Annabelle dance and meet people. That's where she met Mr. Evans. He's real nice, except for those dumb coin tricks."

Wanda smiled. "I don't see nothing wrong with it if it makes Annabelle happy. She might even marry Mr. Evans."

I didn't say anything as we walked up the hill to the house. The thought of my parents dating was too awful

90

for me to think about. Suppose one of them fell in love with somebody else? Then they'd never get back together and I'd have to put up with some weird person who did things like pull quarters out of my ears. It was a horrible thought.

Jason was waiting for us on the front porch. "What's in that bag?" He tried to peep in the grocery bag Wanda was carrying.

Wanda snatched it away. "Nothing for you to see!"

"No potato chips or Fritos or anything?"

"Nope. Just my underwear."

Jason looked disappointed, but he opened the screen door and called, "Aunt Grace, she's here!"

"Hello, Wanda." Aunt Grace came down the hall smiling. "I'm glad you could come."

Wanda smiled, but I rushed past Aunt Grace, afraid of getting trapped in a long, boring conversation. "Come on," I said, "I'll show you where to put your stuff." I ran upstairs, with Wanda behind me.

"You got a pretty room." Wanda walked over to the window and looked out at the darkening sky. "And a pretty view."

"Sometimes I hate it." I stared out at the mountains lying like a dark wall against the sky. "I hate it when it's dark and I don't see any lights out there. Back home there was a streetlight right outside my window and my room never got really dark the way it does here. And there were houses all around with lighted windows and on rainy nights the sky would turn pink from all the neon lights in the shopping center."

Wanda fidgeted with the ruffles on my curtain. "I guess you want to go back there pretty bad, don't you?"

"Do you think I'd go to Maude if I didn't?" I gazed

out at the moon hanging above the mountains like a shiny quarter. "Back home I go swimming every day and there's the mall and the skating rink and the park." My voice trailed off. "And there's my friends," I added softly. "I guess I miss them most of all."

Wanda didn't say anything. She just stood there next to me staring out the window. Finally she looked at me. "If you weren't so interested in running after Maude, I could show you lots of good things to do here. There's a place in the creek where it's deep enough to swim and there's a big municipal pool in Harrisburg. There's even a skating rink and a bowling alley there and I don't know how many food places and stores."

I looked down at the floor, embarrassed. Nothing here was like home. Nothing. I didn't want to go to a pool where I didn't know anybody or swim in a creek. I wanted to go back to Stoneleigh and I wanted my mother and father to live together and I wanted us all to be happy, a big happy normal family.

Wanda picked at the dirt under her fingernails. "Annabelle keeps saying you're homesick, but sometimes I think you're just stuck-up."

Nobody had ever called me stuck-up before and I stared at her, too angry to say anything. It wasn't true. I wasn't stuck-up, just homesick, as Annabelle said.

"Hey." Jason stuck his head through the door and smiled at us. "You want some ice cream? Aunt Grace made some specially for you."

Wanda and I were still glaring at each other. I certainly didn't want any ice cream, especially if I had to eat it with Wanda.

Before I could say anything, Wanda smiled at Jason.

"I'd like some. There's nothing I like better than ice cream."

"It's homemade strawberry and it's yummy, yummy, yummy." Jason rubbed his stomach and smiled.

"From the looks of you, I'm surprised there's any left." I followed Jason and Wanda out of the room, scowling at the ice cream sticking to Jason's hands, arms, legs and feet.

Down in the kitchen, Aunt Grace was scooping up cones of strawberry ice cream. "Let's eat outside on the porch," she said. "It's much cooler out there." She handed us each a cone and we all followed her outside.

"Eat it quickly before it melts," Aunt Grace said, sitting down next to us. Jason climbed onto her lap and we all sat quietly, watching the stars come out and eating our ice cream.

After a while, Aunt Grace turned to Wanda. "I hear Charlene is getting married and going off to Wheeling. I suppose your grandmother will miss her and Tanya Marie."

"She sure will." Wanda probed her cone with her tongue, sucking up the last of her ice cream. "But she's still got me and Mr. Evans. He's her boyfriend." Wanda shot me a look and added, "Do you know where she met him?"

Aunt Grace shook her head.

"At the Adam and Eve Club. You ever been there?"

"I've heard of it, but I've never been there. It's in Harrisburg, isn't it?"

Wanda nodded. "You meet people there, you know, other single people. If you like dancing, it's a good place to find a husband."

Aunt Grace laughed. "Well, I guess I'm out of luck,

93

Wanda. I haven't gone dancing since I was in college and from what I hear, dancing's changed a lot since then. I don't think the Adam and Eve Club is for me."

"You could take dancing lessons. There's a place in Harrisburg that gives lessons. That's where Annabelle went. It cost her a whole lot of money, but she says it was worth every dime." Wanda laughed. "You should see her dance. Why, she's got Charlene beat when it comes to swinging her hips and stuff. She says you get better when you're older. She says Charlene's still worrying about making a fool of herself, but Annabelle's through with worrying about that. All she cares about now is having a good time."

"Well, maybe I'll look into it, Wanda."

"Annabelle will tell you all about it. She says no nice-looking woman ought to be spending all her time alone drawing pictures. Everybody owes it to their self to get out and have a good time once in a while at least. Nobody should waste their self."

Aunt Grace gave Wanda a hug. "Tell Annabelle not to worry about me. I'm doing fine and I'm not wasting a thing."

Wanda looked doubtful and I was afraid she was about to start all over again, so I gave her a little nudge. Then I yawned. "I don't know what's the matter with me, I'm just so tired." I said, trying to look as if I could barely keep my eyes open.

Catching on quickly, Wanda yawned too. "It must be 'cause we helped carry all Charlene's stuff out to the truck," she said.

"Well, maybe the two of you ought to go to bed early then," Aunt Grace said. "I don't want you falling asleep on the porch."

Thanking Aunt Grace for the ice cream, we said good-night and went upstairs to my room. As soon as I shut the door, I turned to Wanda, ready to resume the argument.

"I'm sorry I called you stuck-up," Wanda said, before I had a chance to open my mouth. "I was just kind of mad, I guess."

"You haven't changed your mind about going to Maude's then?"

Wanda shook her head. "I still think it's dumb, but I'll go with you. I said I would and I will."

I smiled at her and she smiled back. Then I turned out the light and we lay down on the bed, pulling the sheet over us to hide our clothes. "See how dark it is in here?" I said.

"No darker than my room." Wanda turned from her back to her side. "This bed sure is creaky."

"I know. It's an antique. You know what gives me the creeps about sleeping in it? People have probably died in it."

"So? People probably got born in it too." Wanda's voice sounded a little uncertain.

"Maybe. But it scares me sometimes if I think about it in the middle of the night."

"Then don't think about it. And don't talk about it either, okay?" Wanda propped herself up on one elbow and frowned at me. "It's bad enough I got to go see Maude without you talking about people dying in the bed I got to sleep in."

"I'm sorry." I lay still for a few minutes, staring at the ceiling. When Wanda didn't say anything, I poked her in the ribs. "You asleep already?"

"Not now I'm not," Wanda said.

"Do you really think my mother and father would go out on dates?"

"Huh?"

"Suppose one of them fell in love with somebody. What would happen to Jason and me?"

"Beats me." Wanda sounded sleepy. "What're your folks like anyway? How come you want your father back so bad?"

"Well, he's, I don't know; he knows how to make me laugh and he's as handsome as a movie star. I'll show you." Getting out of bed, I went to the dresser and found the things I was supposed to give Maude. Switching on my flashlight, I sat down on the bed and showed Wanda the snapshot of my parents. "See what I mean? He's a kind of a combination of Robert Redford and Paul Newman, don't you think?"

Wanda squinted at the picture and nodded. "He sure is good-looking, but you know what they say about good-looking men."

"What?"

"You can't trust them, that's all. Not when they're really good-looking."

"Well, not all of them maybe. But my father's wonderful. He just happens to be good-looking, too. He can't help his looks, can he?"

Wanda drew back a little, as if she sensed I was getting mad, and shrugged her shoulders. "I'm just telling you what people say. I don't know about your father." She looked at the picture again. "Your mother's real pretty. They look like they're on their honeymoon or something, only I can see Jason behind them. How come they're getting a divorce?"

"I don't know. It seems awfully complicated to me,

but I think some of it was Jason's fault in a way, 'cause he never acted the way Daddy wanted him to. You know what a baby he is, how he cries about everything and gets scared, and he can't play any sports. Daddy used to get mad at him and then Mom would get mad at Daddy and before long they'd be in a fight. Then she wanted to go back to college and finish her degree and he didn't want her to and they fought a lot about that. Finally Daddy just couldn't take it anymore and he left. I think Mom could've stopped him, but she didn't, so I kind of blame her for a lot of it."

"What makes you think they don't want a divorce?" Wanda looked at me, her face pale in the dim light from the flashlight.

"I just know. Neither one of them is the type who should live alone, especially Mom. She needs Daddy to take care of her, but she's too proud to admit it. She wants to be like Aunt Grace, independent and self-sufficient and all that stuff, but she's really like Annabelle. She needs a man." I frowned at Mom's smiling face. If she were here right now, I'd tell her myself, I'd force her to see the truth about herself.

"It must be nice to know so much," Wanda said in a huffy little voice. "Not many kids know more about life than their own parents do."

I glared at her and snapped the flashlight off. "It's almost eleven-thirty," I said coldly. "We should leave in about fifteen minutes."

For the next quarter of an hour, neither one of us said a word. We just lay on the bed, watching the numbers flip on my clock radio. At eleven-forty-five, we both got up and tiptoed to the door. The hall was dark, but as we crept past Jason's door, I saw him in the glow of his night-light, sleeping peacefully with his arms around his old teddy bear. There wasn't a sound downstairs except the *tick tock tick* of the grandfather's clock. I led the way down the steps, pausing each time a tread creaked under my feet. We passed Aunt Grace's door, shut tight with no crack of light shining under it.

At the back door, I turned the knob slowly and stepped out onto the porch. Sitting down on the top step, we put on our shoes and ran across the lawn, taking the shortcut across the field.

"Everything looks different in the moonlight," I whispered. "Even the shapes of things."

"Wait till we get in the woods," Wanda said, looking ahead at the dark mass of trees.

"That's why I brought the flashlight." I took it out of the pocket in my sweatshirt and clicked it on. Its beam made a small circle of light on one of the trees.

"Don't do much, do it?" Wanda said.

At the edge of the woods, we paused and shone the flashlight down the path ahead of us. Something rustled in the bushes and we clung to each other for a moment.

"It was just a coon or a possum or something," Wanda said nervously.

"Yeah," I said, looking behind me. "Well, come on."

Following the tunnel of light cast by the flashlight, we crept into the woods like thieves entering a house, scarcely daring to make a sound. Without saying a word to each other, we climbed the path as it twisted uphill, curving around trees and boulders. By the time we reached the top, we were both out of breath.

"That must be her house." Wanda pointed at a ramshackle cabin rising from an outcropping of boulders.

From where we stood, it looked as if it had been put together room by room without any plan. Parts of it were log, parts of it were shingled and parts of it were bare planks. Spooky as it looked, it wasn't surrounded by a bone fence and there wasn't a crumb of gingerbread in sight.

While we stood there staring, Maude emerged from the shadows on the porch and beckoned to us. "I'm so glad you've come, my dears." She crossed the clearing and seized our hands, as if she thought we might change our minds and run. "You didn't find the woods frightening, did you?" She smiled at us, her eyes hidden in shadows. "Come inside with me, my dears, come inside and sit by an old lady's fire."

Wordlessly, we allowed Maude to lead us up her sagging steps and into a small, dark room. In the dim light cast by a fire flickering on the hearth, I saw bunches of dried herbs hanging from the rafters, a table heaped with books and papers, shelves crowded with bottles, jars, and more books. On the mantelpiece, a stuffed owl peered down at me, its glass eyes glittering in the firelight, and next to him Soot perched, twisting his head from side to side as he looked from Wanda to me and back again. "Krrrrk?" he asked. "Krrrrk?"

The cabin was exactly as I had thought it would be, and I felt as if I'd stepped out of the real world and into a fairy tale. In the corners, the shadows thickened into inky darkness, and as Maude turned and smiled at me, her face masked with shadows, she seemed full of mystery and menace.

"Yes, Soot, we have company tonight," Maude said. "Laura Adams is here. Shall I help her, my dear? Shall I do all I can in memory of Margaret?"

The crow nodded its head and shifted about. Once more he turned his yellow eyes toward me and stared, unblinking, as if he could read every thought.

Maude smiled and nodded. "Sit down, Laura Adams. And you too, Wanda." She led us to a semicircle of three chairs facing the huge stone fireplace. She chose the middle chair for herself, a tall armchair painted black and decorated with elaborate carvings of strange beasts. Wanda and I sat on either side of her, in smaller versions of the same chair.

For a moment all was still. The fire sputtered and crackled, shooting sparks up the chimney, and a gust of wind set the pines moaning outside the cabin. The air was heavy with the musky sweet smell of incense. As the firelight played on the chairs, the carved beasts seemed to stretch and blink and peer about the room, their eyes gleaming with life. I shivered, wishing I'd taken Wanda's advice and stayed home.

"And have you brought what I asked you to, Laura Adams?" Maude leaned toward me, her hand outstretched to receive the things I took from my pocket.

The old woman smiled as she looked at the photograph. "How happy your parents look, how young and healthy. Were you at the ocean?"

I nodded. "It was last year. Before Daddy left." I stared at the picture wishing my parents hadn't posed especially for the picture, wishing they really were happy together, wishing the photograph were true.

"And this is your aunt's brush? What a fine artist she must be, what pleasure painting must give her." Putting the brush aside, Maude examined the little car. "And this must belong to Jason." She smiled at me and nodded her head. "You have done well, Laura, very well. These things will make my job very easy. You cannot imagine how grateful I am to you for giving me this opportunity to help Margaret's beloved ones."

Getting up from her chair, Maude bent over a cauldron hanging above the fire. She picked up a ladle and began stirring the contents of the cauldron. As sweet fumes arose from the pot, Wanda and I stood up to watch. I had trouble concentrating on what Maude was doing, but I thought I saw her pass the things I'd given her back and forth through the flames, murmuring softly to herself.

Leaning forward, I saw the photograph slowly curl and turn black at the corners. The smiling faces shrivelled and turned old and ugly. The paint on Jason's car bubbled, the hairs on the brush burned, but before everything crumbled into ashes, Maude put the charred remains into a small box and closed the lid. She wrapped the box round and round with fine threads, still chanting and gesturing.

The smoke from the cauldron grew denser, swirling around me like green fog and making it impossible for me to see anything clearly. I started feeling dizzy and light-headed, the shadows in the corners swayed, the room spun, and I felt as if I were about to fall. Terrified, I reached out for Wanda's hand, but grabbed Maude's hand instead.

"Now, now, my dear, it's quite all right." Maude gripped my hand tightly, chilling me to the bone. "In a moment the air will clear and you'll feel fine."

As Maude spoke, the smoke thinned and trailed up the chimney, leaving a sweet aroma behind. I stared at Wanda, noticing that Maude held her hand too. "Is that all?" I whispered, hoping that we were free to leave.

"In such a hurry to rush off and leave me?" Maude smiled at me, her eyes reflecting the fire. "My, my, Laura Adams, you make it very clear that you come to me for business only, not for friendship." She chuckled and released my hand. "Yes, you may go now, both of you. By tomorrow night your parents will be here, united this time forever, Laura."

"Thank you," I whispered, still feeling dizzy from the fumes. "Thank you very much."

"Thank *you*, Laura Adams, for making something possible that I've dreamed about for years. Eh, Soot? Isn't it true that we've waited a long time, my lovely?"

The old woman looked up at the crow, who stirred on his perch and nodded his head. "You see? Soot knows how much this means to me. Soon you will know, too, Laura Adams."

I stared at her, no longer sure what she was talking about, and Wanda gave me a nudge toward the door.

"Be sure and give Grace Randall my love," Maude called as we stepped outside. "Tell her she should have told you about me and Margaret. Tell her she has only herself to blame, my dear."

Before I could ask what she meant by that, Maude, still chuckling, closed the door, leaving Wanda and me on the porch.

"Come on, Laura, let's get out of here!" Without looking to see if I were following, Wanda leaped off the porch and ran across the clearing.

chapter

~12~

When I woke up in the morning, Aunt Grace was leaning over the bed, shaking my shoulder, her face worried. Confused by dreams and Maude's words, I stared at her. "Are they here already?" I asked.

"It's Jason. He's very sick, Laura. I've called Doctor Benson and I thought I'd get you up before he comes." Aunt Grace looked at Wanda as if she'd forgotten who she was, but Wanda went on sleeping peacefully despite the sun shining in her eyes.

"What's wrong with Jason?" I slid out of bed, trying not to disturb Wanda.

"I don't know. He woke up early complaining that his head hurt. I took his temperature and it was over a hundred and three."

"Is that high?"

Aunt Grace nodded. "I hate to send Wanda home without any breakfast, but Doctor Benson will be here any minute. Do you think you could fix something for yourselves?"

"Sure. We can just have cereal and toast or something. You know me. I never eat breakfast anyway." I saw Wanda open one eye and look around the room. "Come on, Wanda, time to get up."

I tweaked at the covers, then looked back at Aunt Grace. "Don't worry about Jason. He gets sick all the time to get attention. Do you know he's been sick on every birthday I've had since he was born? And on every vacation too. The last time we went to Ocean City, he burst his eardrum and we had to take him to the emergency room."

Aunt Grace shook her head. "I don't think anyone could have a fever that high on purpose, Laura." She smiled at Wanda, who was now sitting up, looking totally confused. Wanda's hair stuck up in spikes all over her head and her cheek had a long crease mark on it from her pillow. "Jason's sick, Wanda. I'm expecting Doctor Benson soon, so I'll leave you two to get dressed."

We were sitting at the kitchen table eating toast and applesauce when Doctor Benson arrived. We heard him say a few words to Aunt Grace in the hall before going upstairs. Overhead his footsteps were loud as he walked around in Jason's room.

"He doesn't usually come to people's houses," Wanda said. "Not unless they got something really wrong with them."

"Maybe he likes Aunt Grace." I toyed with my toast and giggled. "Maybe she's his girlfriend."

Wanda shook her head, her face serious. "Aren't you worried about your brother?"

"I told you he makes himself sick on purpose." I picked up Aunt Grace's cat. "Are you hungry, Thomas? Do you want some applesauce, Mister KittyCat?" Thomas pulled away from my bowl and tried to leap out of my arms. "I bet Jason got Aunt Grace so distracted she forgot to feed you."

Letting the cat go, I looked at Wanda. She was just sitting there, staring at me as if I were some kind of a monster. We were both very aware of the footsteps overhead, of the low murmur of voices, of Jason's absence. Despite what I'd just said, I was worried about my brother. Suppose he was really sick?

Wanda got up and carried her dishes to the sink. "Maybe I should get on home," she said, but before she'd finished rinsing them, Doctor Benson came downstairs. Paying no attention to either one of us, he picked up the telephone receiver and started dialing.

"Yes, Doctor Benson here," he said. "Have you got a room available in Isolation?"

There was a pause. I stared at the doctor, my heart beating quicker. "Good," he said. "I'll be there in about half an hour with a child. Looks like meningitis, so get ready for a spinal tap." There was another pause. "Jason Adams. Five years old." Pause. "Fine. See you soon."

Hanging up the phone, he looked at me for the first time. "I'm taking your brother to the hospital." He gave me what was probably meant to be a reassuring smile. "He'll be all right, don't worry. I'll take good care of him."

Before I could say a word, Aunt Grace appeared in the doorway with Jason in her arms. His face was flushed scarlet and he stared at me as if he'd never seen me before.

"Mommy," Jason whimpered. "Daddy."

"Laura, we have to leave right now. Jason needs immediate care. I'm going to phone your mother and father from the hospital, so please stay here in case they call. I'll call you as soon as we get Jason settled."

"Everything will be all right." Doctor Benson patted me on the shoulder and followed Aunt Grace outside.

"Mommy, Daddy, Mommy, Daddy," Jason cried. "It hurts, it hurts."

Wanda and I went outside too and watched them get into Doctor Benson's car. Wordlessly we watched the big Buick until it rounded a curve in the road and disappeared. It seemed very quiet. A bird sang in the woods across the road, a breeze ruffled the leaves of the maple tree, and a cricket cheeped under the porch.

"Is he going to be okay?" Wanda stared at me, her eyes full of worry.

"I don't know." I felt weak and trembly and dangerously close to throwing up my breakfast. "He wasn't faking," I said, feeling my eyes fill with tears. "He wasn't faking at all, and I didn't even go in to see him before the doctor came. Suppose he dies and I didn't even say good-bye to him?"

Wanda touched my arm gently. "He'll be okay, Laura. I just know it. Doctor Benson's a wonderful doctor, just like the ones on 'General Hospital,' Annabelle says."

I sat down on the steps and Thomas, hungry for breakfast, rubbed up against me, purring like a little motorboat. Nearby, Wanda leaned against the porch railing, examining the mosquito bites on her arms.

"You want me to stay till your aunt comes back?" Wanda asked.

I nodded. I didn't want to be by myself.

After a long time, the phone rang and I ran to answer it, hoping it was Mom or Dad. I was disappointed to hear Aunt Grace's voice and I braced myself for bad news.

"They aren't sure what's wrong with him, Laura. It looks like meningitis but so far the test are inconclusive." Aunt Grace sounded so worried that I started shaking. "I've called your parents and they should be here in about three hours or so. Can you get along all right till then? I don't want to leave Jason until your parents arrive."

"Is he worse?" I whispered.

"No. He's about the same. He just keeps calling for your mother and father." Aunt Grace's voice trailed off and I heard her blow her nose.

"He won't die, will he?"

"Of course not, Laura. Don't think such things." Aunt Grace's voice sounded funny, as if she didn't really believe what she was saying. "He's a fine healthy little boy. Yesterday there wasn't a thing wrong with him. He's going to be all right, Laura, I'm sure of it."

If she was so sure of it, why did she have to keep saying it? After I said good-bye, I went back into the living room and sat down on the couch next to Wanda.

"Is he better?" Wanda asked.

I shook my head. "If anyone dies, it should be me," I said. "I'm the mean one, I deserve it, not Jason."

"That's dumb." Wanda frowned at me. "Nobody deserves to die."

"You don't think this happened because of going to see Maude, do you?" I asked Wanda.

"How could Maude make Jason sick? She hasn't been anywhere near him." Wanda looked puzzled.

"Witches can put hexes on people," I said. "They've got all kinds of ways to do it."

"They only do that to people they got a grudge against. Maude hasn't any reason to harm Jason. She was your grandmother's friend. You heard her say so yourself, Laura."

"But she said my mother and father would be here tonight and they're on their way right now. They wouldn't be coming if Jason weren't sick."

Wanda shook her head. "Eddie came back to Charlene and there wasn't anybody sick. Both Charlene and Tanya Marie was as healthy as cows. No, him getting sick is just a coincidence."

"In Salem they wouldn't have thought so. They'd have arrested Maude and put her on trial and probably burned her at the stake."

"Well, nobody does things like that anymore." Wanda folded her arms across her chest and stretched out her long, skinny legs.

I knew Wanda well enough to know she didn't want to talk about Maude, so I didn't say anything. I just sat there worrying about Jason and, at the same time, looking forward to seeking Mom and Dad. Who knows, I told myself, maybe this really would be the thing to bring my parents to their senses. Maybe Maude knew that making Jason a little bit sick was the only way to get them up here. As long as he wasn't in too much pain and got well fast once they got here, maybe it would all be for the best.

Late in the afternoon I heard a car drive up to the house. I jumped up and looked out the window. Aunt Grace was getting out of Daddy's car, but he wasn't driving. A woman I'd never seen before was sitting behind the steering wheel. Mystified, I ran outside to meet them, with Wanda following behind.

"Where's Daddy?" I asked Aunt Grace.

"He's still at the hospital, he and your mother both."

"Is Jason better?"

"I think seeing Andrea and George perked him up a little, but he's still very sick. The doctors don't know what's wrong with him." Aunt Grace shook her head and then turned to the woman standing beside her, who was smiling uncertainly at me. "Oh, Laura, this is Carol Carmack, your father's secretary."

I stared at Carol, taking in her perfectly made-up face, her long blonde hair feathered back professionally, her tight jeans, her pale pink T-shirt. She looked like a fashion model, the kind you see photographed on beautiful beaches in the Caribbean, riding a horse in the surf and smiling into the sunset. I hated her at first sight. Couldn't somebody ugly type Daddy's letters and answer his phone?

"I'm so glad to meet you, Laura. I've heard so much about you." Carol smiled widely, showing even more of her beautiful teeth. "She looks just like George, doesn't she?"

Aunt Grace shrugged. "I've always thought she favored Andrea myself."

I smiled at Aunt Grace, thinking that was a pretty good put-down. Out of the corner of my eye I glanced at Wanda to see how she was reacting to all this. She smirked at me and winked. For some reason, the knowing look in her eye worried me.

"Would you like a cup of tea?" Aunt Grace asked Carol. Her voice was polite, but she could just as well have been offering her a cup of turpentine, I thought.

I started to follow them inside, but Wanda grabbed my arm. "I knew it!" she hissed.

"Knew what?" I pulled away, not sure I wanted to hear what Wanda was dying to tell me.

"I knew your daddy must have a girlfriend!"

"She's not his girlfriend, she's his secretary. You heard what Aunt Grace said." I scowled at Wanda. "He's a lawyer and he has a lot of paperwork to do. He used to bring it home every night. Some nights he had so much work he couldn't come home at all!"

Wanda shook her head. "She don't look like no secretary to me."

"Shut up, Wanda! What do you know about lawyers and secretaries and things like that?"

"More than you know about girlfriends, that's for sure!"

"Get out of here!" I swung at Wanda with my open hand, meaning to slap her right off the porch, but she ducked and I almost fell into the chinaberry bush.

"What's going on?" Aunt Grace peered at us through the screen door.

"I'm just going home, that's all!" Wanda ran down the steps and across the lawn.

"What was that all about?" Aunt Grace stared at me. "You didn't quarrel with Wanda, did you?"

"She thinks she knows everything!" I pushed past Aunt Grace into the hall. "What's *she* doing here? Why didn't she stay in Washington?"

"Who, Carol? Your father said he had so much work to do, he needed her to help him in the evenings, so he brought her along."

"Well, why didn't she stay at the hospital?"

"For some reason, her presence upset Jason. To make

110

things easier, I suggested she drive me back here. I couldn't just leave her in Harrisburg."

"How are Mom and Dad getting back here without the car?"

"In your mother's car, Laura."

"You mean they didn't drive up here together?" I stared at Aunt Grace.

"Honey, they don't live together anymore. They each drove up. Your father and Carol, your mother by herself." Aunt Grace gave me a little hug. "Why don't you come have a cup of tea with Carol and me?"

Not being able to think of anything better to do, I followed Aunt Grace back to the kitchen and sat down at the table with Carol.

"Hi." She smiled at me as if she was doing me a favor. "What happened to your sidekick?"

"She went home." I busied myself measuring honey into my tea, hoping she'd take the hint and stop talking to me.

"Do you mind if I smoke?" Carol looked at Aunt Grace and smiled as if she were a cute little girl asking to be excused for having a bad habit.

"Not if you don't mind sitting out on the back porch." Aunt Grace smiled too, but I could tell she wasn't about to excuse any bad habits Carol might have.

Carol looked a little surprised. "Oh, you noble non-smokers! You sure make it hard for us sinners." She laughed. "You used to be able to smoke just about anywhere, except church, but now all you see are those awful little No Smoking signs. I'm getting so I'm ashamed to light up." She laughed again and stood up. "Would you like to keep me company in exile, Laura?"

I looked from her to Aunt Grace, not sure what to

say. I didn't want to be rude exactly, but I felt uncomfortable around Carol. "I guess so."

"Well, I'd better get something started for dinner." Aunt Grace got up and opened the refrigerator.

"Do you need any help?" I surprised myself by volunteering my services.

"After a while you can set the table," Aunt Grace said.

"Did you paint this?" Carol stopped at the drawing table and stared at an unfinished painting of a squirrel perched on the limb of a pine tree. "George told me you were an artist, but I had no idea you were this good. This squirrel's so cute! Walt Disney himself couldn't have painted a better one."

"It's not finished." Aunt Grace didn't bother to look up from the lettuce she was rinsing.

"Well, it's just adorable. Do you have any others I could look at?" Carol persisted.

"No. They're all packed and ready to send to a gallery in Boston."

Carol looked impressed. "Do you sell a lot of art work?"

"Enough to buy groceries and pay my electric bill." Aunt Grace bent down and opened the cupboard where she kept her pots and pans. She made so much noise rummaging around for what she wanted that Thomas got up from the windowsill where he'd been napping. He stretched and walked off, tail in the air, obviously displeased at having been so rudely awakened.

"Well, I've got to have my coffin nail. Coming, Laura?" Carol opened the door and held it for me as I followed her outside.

Just as we were running out of things to say about the weather and the scenery, we saw Mom's car turn into the driveway.

"They're here!" I jumped off the porch and raced across the lawn to meet them, not caring whether Carol got left behind or not.

"Laura! Oh, honey, you look wonderful!" Smiling happily, Mom threw her arms around me.

"Mom! Mom!" I hugged her tightly, happy to feel her familiar bony frame and to smell the fragrance her shampoo always left in her hair.

"Darling!" Over Mom's shoulder, I saw Daddy walking toward me, his hair tousled, his smile warm. Up and down my spine I felt all tingly with happiness at the sight of him.

As I pulled away from Mom to hug him, he grabbed me around the waist and tried to swing me up in the air. "Hey," he grunted in surprise, "do you have ten pound weights in your shoes or something?"

I shook my head, laughing happily.

"Well, it must be the mountain air. Or your aunt's cooking. Anyway, you're prettier than ever!"

Aunt Grace waved from the door. "Come on, you all. I've got dinner on the table."

As soon as we sat down, I could feel the tension. Mom sat between Aunt Grace and me, Dad sat on my other side, and Carol sat between him and Aunt Grace. No one said anything as Aunt Grace passed the chicken around. No one looked at each other. The only sound was the clink of forks. It was so quiet I could hear myself chewing.

"Is Jason any better?" I said suddenly.

Mom shook her head. "He's about the same, honey. They're still not sure what's wrong with him." She pushed her plate away, leaving a drumstick and half her potato salad untouched.

"I think we should take him back to Washington. I'm

sure the doctors at Children's Hospital would know what to do." Dad frowned at Mom. "What can you expect from a hospital in the middle of nowhere?"

"I told you I agree with Doctor Benson. Jason is too sick to travel, George." Mom returned Dad's frown. "He's better off here. They're doing all they can."

"Well, it's not enough." Dad's voice rose a notch, and my stomach churned. Why did they always argue at the dinner table?

Mom looked at Aunt Grace. "Is that hammock out on the porch comfortable?"

"It's wonderful. Go out and try it, Andrea. You'll love it." Aunt Grace smiled and gave Mom a pat as she left the table.

As soon as Mom was out of the room, Dad turned to Aunt Grace. "Well, how's life in West Virginia?"

"Great." Aunt Grace smiled at him and helped herself to more salad. As she passed the bowl to Carol, she added, "I love it here."

"But don't you get bored sometimes? Why, Blue Hollow doesn't even have a restaurant, let alone a movie theater, and it's a half hour's drive to Harrisburg."

Aunt Grace shrugged. "A great cook like me doesn't need to eat out and the mountains are more interesting to watch than most movies are."

"It really is beautiful up here." Carol smiled and waved her fork vaguely at the window and the mountains stretching away to the sky. "And the way she paints." She chewed a mouthful of salad. "If I could paint like that, I'd never be bored."

Dad smiled at Carol and shrugged. "Well, Grace, as long as you're happy, I suppose that's all that matters. But frankly I prefer the city."

I looked at Daddy. "You told me you'd give anything to spend a whole summer in the mountains, soaking up sunshine and breathing fresh air. You said I was really lucky to be coming up here!"

Dad laughed and ruffled my hair as if I were five years old. "Laura, I'm talking about spending your whole life in a place like this. I'd love to get away from Washington for a summer, but I wouldn't want to move up here permanently."

Ignoring Dad, Aunt Grace turned to me. "Do you want more chicken, Laura?"

I shook my head. The way my stomach felt, I didn't think I'd want food for a week or more. "No, thanks," I said, "but I'll help you clear the table." Picking up Carol's plate and mine, I carried them to the sink.

After we washed the dishes, Aunt Grace and I went out on the porch. Mom was lying in the hammock, gazing out across the valley at the sunset, and Dad and Carol were sitting on the steps, laughing at something Dad had just said. I sat down next to Daddy and leaned my head against his shoulder, breathing in the familiar scent of his after-shave lotion.

"Hi, sweetie." Daddy gave me a little hug and ruffled my hair again. "Get the kitchen in good shape?"

I nodded. "Of course. I'm an expert at cleaning up. Just think of all the times I've cleaned up your kitchen."

Dad laughed, but Carol leaned around him, smiling, and said, "Isn't he the worst slob? Cleaning up after him is like cleaning up after a two-year-old!"

I stared at her. How did she know what Daddy's kitchen looked like? Or did she mean his office was a mess too? "I thought you were his secretary, not his maid," I said, frowning at her.

Her face flushed and she laughed, but before she could say anything, Daddy stood up and stretched. "Boy, it sure is a beautiful evening. Why don't we go for a walk?"

Carol and I both got up, but it was Carol Daddy spoke to. "Where would you like to go? Down through the woods to the creek or just along the road?"

Looking down at her sandals, Carol shrugged. "I think along the road would be best. These aren't exactly walking shoes."

"Are you coming too?" Daddy turned to me, and there was something in his tone of voice that said he hoped I wasn't.

I hesitated, trying to decide whether to go just to spite him or to say no and sulk. Aunt Grace intervened before I could say anything. "Why don't you stay here and keep your Mom and me company?"

In the few seconds it took me to decide, Dad and Carol started walking across the lawn, their shadows stretching out behind them, long and thin, pinheaded, reaching almost to my feet. I started to go after them, but Aunt Grace caught my arm. "Come on, Laura, sit down and have a glass of iced tea with us."

Angrily I pulled away from her and looked at Mom. She was still sitting in the hammock, adjusting the strap on her sandal, as if it were extremely important to get it just right. Turning my back on both of them, I sat down on the porch railing and watched Dad and Carol disappear around the curve in the road. Even from this distance I could hear Carol laughing, soft and silvery like a teenager.

Aunt Grace went inside and brought out a tray of iced tea glasses. I took mine and sat where I was, my back to her and Mom, staring at the road and half-hoping I'd see Wanda come into sight. Behind me, I could hear the clink of ice in glasses and the soft voices of my mother and my aunt, talking about Jason. Gradually the conversation shifted away from my brother and I heard Mom ask Aunt Grace about Maude.

"No, I haven't seen her for quite a while. When I first moved here, I used to see her nearly every day. She'd stop down there in the road and stare at the house till she saw me, then she'd wave her fist and curse at me. It was quite embarrassing, really, not to mention kind of sad. Poor old soul."

"She hasn't bothered Jason or Laura, has she?"

"Laura saw her one night in the road, going through her old routine in front of the house, but I told her not to worry about it. Every town has a borderline lunatic like Maude."

"You really think she's harmless?" Mom's voice sounded so uncertain I turned around to look at her. That was a mistake of course, because they both stopped talking and looked at each other, obviously relaying an adult message that meant I wasn't old enough to hear any more about Maude.

"You don't need to stop talking on account of me," I said. "I know all about Maude. She's a witch; everybody around here knows that."

I tried to look as blasé as possible because I wanted very much to hear more about Maude. All day long I'd been worrying about her, trying to decide what I should do about Jason. I wanted my parents to be here, but I was uneasy about a couple of things; one, of course, was Jason himself. I didn't like his being sick, especially if my visit to Maude was responsible for it. I also was uneasy about Carol and the way she seemed to come between Daddy and Mom. With her here, I didn't see how they were going to make up and decide they loved each other.

"Laura, I told you that Maude is just an old woman, a little crazy but no more a witch than you or I," Aunt Grace said.

"She hasn't said anything to you, has she?" Mom asked.

I shrugged. "I've only seen her a couple of times," I said evasively.

"I'd stay away from her if I were you," Mom said.

"Why? Do you think she's going to put me in a cage and fatten me up for Sunday dinner?" I tried to make it sound like a joke, but I don't think I succeeded. There was something in my mother's voice that made me uneasy, some secret she was keeping from me.

"She's a strange old woman, Laura, and she has a grudge against our family. I don't trust her and I don't want you to go near her." Mom looked at Aunt Grace. "I think you should've told her about Maude. Saying she's just a harmless old eccentric isn't enough, Grace."

"Oh, Andrea, you surely wouldn't have wanted me to scare Laura with all that superstitious nonsense? I didn't want her to spend the whole summer here cowering in the yard, afraid to step off this property for fear of meeting Maude. I still resent Grandmother's scaring us half to death with her Maude stories when we were children."

"What are you talking about? What Maude stories? Why were you scared of her?" My heart pounding, I leaned forward, my eyes on my mother. "Tell me, I want to know!"

118

"It all started with your grandmother," Mom said.

As she paused, obviously wondering where to begin, I interrupted. "With Grandmother? I thought Maude and Grandmother were friends."

"Friends? Where did you get that idea?" Aunt Grace stared at me, puzzled.

Feeling a little shaky, I said, "Maude told me; she said I looked just like Grandmother, that seeing me reminded her of their friendship, that she wanted to—" I paused, stopping myself just in time. "She wanted to be my friend," I finished lamely.

"Well, they *were* friends once," Aunt Grace said, smiling at Mom. "Maybe Maude finally decided to forgive and forget. People often mellow as they get older."

"How can you say that?" Mom stared at Aunt Grace. "She told Mother she'd never forgive her and she meant it. You know that Grandmother always blamed her for Mother's death." Mom's voice rose and she got up from the hammock. Pacing around nervously, she added, "And Grandmother said Maude had sworn revenge on all of us, that she said she'd make us all sorry someday."

"Calm down, Andrea, you're scaring Laura. Look at her. She's as white as the frosting on a wedding cake." Aunt Grace put her hand on Mom's shoulder. "Why don't you go lie down for a while? This has been an exhausting day for you."

Mom shook her head and pulled away from Aunt Grace. "Tell Laura about Maude, tell her now. I want her to know why I'm afraid of her. I want her to know why she should stay away from her." Mom sat down on the railing next to me and put an arm around my shoulders.

Aunt Grace sighed and leaned against the railing on the other side of me. It was dark now. The stars were out and the moon hung low over the mountains. Behind me, in the tall grass in the field, a chorus of insects chirped and peeped, and the night air felt cool on my bare arms. But the goose bumps on my skin came from my mother's fear, not from the breeze.

"First of all," Aunt Grace went on, "When your grandmother and Maude were little girls, they were good friends, absolutely inseparable, but as they grew into their teens, Maude got more and more moody. She'd always been very emotional and very domineering. Your grandmother followed her around like a little puppy, doing everything Maude wanted her to do, but she found it harder and harder to get along with Maude. Finally she started avoiding her, and Maude spent more and more time alone, wandering about in the woods by herself, isolating herself from other people, getting stranger and stranger.

"Then Mother heard rumors that Maude had apprenticed herself to an old woman up in the hills who claimed to be a witch. That scared Mother and she stopped seeing Maude altogether." Aunt Grace smiled at Mom. "Do you really want me to go on with this nonsense? I feel so silly talking about it."

Mom nodded, tightening her arm around me. "Tell her about Dad," she said.

Aunt Grace sighed. "Well, probably nothing more would have happened between Mother and Maude if they hadn't both fallen in love with the same man. Your grandfather. When he married Mom, Maude was furious. She visited the house the night before the wedding and made a horrible scene, vowing all sorts of things and forcing Grandmother to call the sheriff just to get her out of the house. It must have been like a scene from a fairy tale. At any rate, Mom and Dad left Blue Hollow after the wedding and never came back." Aunt Grace shrugged. "What else is there to say?"

"That Mom and Dad were killed in an automobile crash on their eighth anniversary," Mom said, "and that Grandmother always blamed Maude for their deaths."

"Andrea, you know how superstitious Grandmother was. You're scaring Laura half to death with all this talk about witchcraft. She's trembling." Aunt Grace patted my knee. "Maude's full of spite and ill will, but she's no more capable of putting a curse on someone than I am."

I shook my head, too upset to say anything. What had I done? I'd never felt comfortable around Maude; I'd never really trusted her, yet I'd gone to her house and helped her cast a spell for me. What was I going to do? How could I make Maude undo the spell?

Without saying good-night, I slid off the porch railing and ran upstairs to bed.

chapter

~<13>~

Unable to sleep, I lay curled in a ball under my covers, trying not to think about Maude and Jason. But all I saw when I closed my eyes was Maude bending over me smiling, her cold hand gripping my arm, her eyes probing mine, offering her help and lying to me, deceiving me, tricking me into betraying my own family.

Was Jason going to die? If he did, it would be all my fault. I would be a murderer, my own brother's killer. It was a thought so horrible, I began to cry, burying my face in the pillow so no one would hear me and ask me what was wrong.

Just as I was about to fall asleep, my door opened and I sat up, half expecting to see Maude standing by my bed.

"Why, Laura, I thought you'd be asleep by now." Mom sat down on my bed and I threw myself at her, holding her tight, tears running down my face.

"Laura, Laura, what is it? What's wrong?" Mom hugged me and patted me the way she used to when I was little. "Did you have a bad dream, honey?"

"Is Jason going to die, Mommy? Is he?" I sobbed.

"No, Laura, no. I'm sure he's going to get well." She held me so tight I could hardly breathe, but I could hear the fear in her voice.

"Why don't they know what's wrong with him?"

Mom shook her head. "One of the doctors thinks it could be a rare virus of some sort, hard to identify." Her voice trailed off indecisively and she stroked my hair back from my face. "He'll be all right, I know he will."

"But suppose someone put a curse on him? Can doctors cure curses?"

"Oh, Laura, Grace was right. I never should have made her bring up that stuff about Maude. We really frightened you, didn't we?" Mom looked at me closely, her face pale and worried.

Picking at a design in my quilt, I said, "But you told Aunt Grace you believed it; you said your grandmother thought Maude made your parents get killed. Couldn't Maude put a curse on Jason?"

Mom shivered. "Let's not think about it, Laura." Looking past me at the black night outside my window, she shook her head. "Spells, witchcraft, it's too much on top of everything else. I can't deal with it, Laura, I can't."

Cuddling closer to her, I grasped her hand. "Will you stroke my arm till I fall asleep the way you did when I was little?"

"Of course." Mom took my arm and stroked it lightly with her fingertips, up and down, soft and gentle. "Do you want me to sing too?" she whispered. "I still know the words to 'Now the Day is Over.' "

"No, you don't have to sing, but I wish you could sleep here with me."

She smiled. "Just relax and go to sleep, Laura. If you need me, I'll be right down the hall."

She kept on stroking my arm, stroking and stroking, till I began to relax and feel safe. I must have drifted off to sleep while she sat on my bed, because I never knew when she stopped stroking my arm or when she left my room.

When I woke up, the sun was shining in my eyes and the house was quiet. No Jason talking in the kitchen, no Jason running up the stairs to wake me, no Jason asking me to help him button his overall straps or tie his shoes. Missing him, I dressed quickly and ran downstairs, suddenly afraid that something awful might have happened while I was asleep.

"Good morning, Laura." Aunt Grace was sitting at the table drinking a cup of coffee. "Your mother and father have already gone to the hospital and Carol is still sleeping. Do you want something to eat?"

I shook my head. "Just juice and coffee." Pouring myself a glassful of orange juice, I sat down across from my aunt. "Jason isn't worse, is he?"

She shook her head. "I don't think so. Your mother said she'd call me around eleven and let me know how he's doing."

I stared at the ceiling at a circle of light, trying to figure out what it was bouncing off. Moving a few things around, I decided it must be the shiny top of the salt shaker. I slid the shaker back and forth on the table, watching the circle of light dart across the ceiling.

Aunt Grace distracted me from my little game, by getting up, coffee mug in hand. "I'm going to have a refill, Laura. How about you?"

"No, thanks." I turned the shaker upside down and sprinkled a few grains of salt on the tabletop. Pushing them about with the tip of my finger, I made little patterns, swirls and circles, wondering all the time what I could do about Maude.

"Well, I guess everybody was an early bird except me." Carol entered the kitchen, as perfectly made-up as she had been the night before. She was wearing a light blue polo shirt with an alligator sewn on the front and a pair of white jeans. "Mmmmm, that coffee smells just wonderful." She smiled as Aunt Grace handed her a steaming mug.

Although Aunt Grace was wearing her hair piled in a knot on the top of her head, a faded pair of Levi's, and an old blue work shirt, I thought she looked much more interesting than Carol. Maybe it was her bones or the little wrinkles around her eyes.

"You look so cute this morning, Laura," Carol said as she sat down next to me. "You're so lucky to have all that natural curl in your hair. You'll never need a permanent or anything."

I forced myself to smile at her as I got up to rinse my coffee mug. Just then the phone rang.

"That must be your mom." Aunt Grace picked up the receiver.

Although she didn't say much more than yes, I knew it was bad news. I could tell by the expression on her face, by the way she held the phone, by her tone of voice.

"He's worse, isn't he?" I asked as she hung up. Don't let him be dead, don't let him be dead, I prayed silently, vowing I'd go to Maude's at once and tell her to make him better.

Aunt Grace shook her head. "He's not really worse,

but he isn't better either and they still don't know what's wrong with him. Nothing they do seems to have any effect." Ignoring Carol's little clucks of sympathy, Aunt Grace sat down at her drawing table and stared at the picture of the squirrel, still unfinished. "What's really bothering your mother is Jason's incessant begging that she and your father stay married. He keeps saying, 'Don't get a divorce, don't get a divorce.' Andrea doesn't know what to do. She thought you all had adjusted to the divorce, that you understood."

I shook my head, not knowing what to say. I didn't want to think about Jason lying in a hospital bed, sick and scared, begging Mom and Dad to love each other. It was horrible. Edging toward the door, I told her I was going over to Wanda's for a while.

Aunt Grace looked a little puzzled, but she let me go. Not wanting to waste any time, I took the shortcut through the woods. If I hadn't been in such a hurry, I probably would have seen Maude step out from the trees in front of me, but I was going so fast I had no chance to avoid her. Skidding to a stop to prevent myself from crashing into her, I stared at her, my knees weak, still panting from running.

"Well, well, Laura Adams, we meet again, and in the sun's light." Maude chuckled and grasped my arm and Soot peered at me from her shoulder. "As I promised, I've brought your parents together, have I not? Your wish is about to come true, my dear, just as I said it would."

"You made Jason sick to do it," I whispered. "I didn't want you to do that."

She chuckled. "It was the only way, Laura. They don't love each other, your mother and father, but they'll stay together now because of Jason. Like ivy binding two trees together, he'll hold them till they rot. And they'll be miserable, Laura, miserable. They'll hate each other more and more every day till there's nothing left of them but their hate."

I tried to pull away, but her grip was too strong. "Not so fast, Laura Adams, not so fast! Aren't you going to thank me for making your wish come true?"

"Please undo it, please!" I cried.

"No, no, what's done cannot be undone, Laura Adams!" She stepped closer to me. "Do you know how long I've waited for this moment? Over fifty years. Since your grandmother took John Randall away from me, I've waited for my revenge. If I'd had the power then that I have now, she'd never have gotten him. He would have married me!"

Maude chuckled. "She didn't have him long, though, did she? It took me eight years, but I got her, and now I'm going to see all her descendants suffer too. Your mother will be chained to a man who doesn't love her and your aunt will never paint again. Her skill is gone along with the brush you stole. And Jason will never recover; crippled for life he'll be. And you, Laura, what's your punishment to be, eh?"

She shook me and then let go of me so quickly that I reeled away from her and fell into the bushes beside the path. As I scrambled to my feet, she smiled at me. "Knowing you made my revenge possible is your punishment, Laura Adams." She bowed her head, still smiling. "Thank you, my dear, thank you so much."

Chuckling, Maude stepped into the woods and disappeared, leaving me standing alone in the middle of the path.

"No!" I screamed after her. "No! You have to undo it, you have to!"

Overhead a crow cawed, loud and mockingly. There was no other answer.

Forgetting my fear, I plunged into the woods after her, heedless of brambles clawing my bare legs and catching in my hair, ignoring the branches slapping my face. "Come back! Come back!" I cried, begging her to stop, to make Jason well, to forgive our family.

Although the woods rang with my cries, there was no answer. Once or twice, I thought I saw her, toiling along ahead of me, slowly and steadily, but it was never Maude I saw. Only a twisted tree hung with vines or a tall rock shaggy with ferns and moss. Never the old woman herself. Like a true witch, she seemed to have vanished, leaving no sign behind.

When I was too tired to go on, I collapsed against a tree and sobbed. I didn't care whether I lived or died and I couldn't bear the thought of going home to my aunt. If Wanda hadn't found me, lying in the ferns at the foot of the tree, I don't know what would have happened to me.

"There must be something you can do, Laura, there must be!" Wanda ran her hands through her hair, ruffling it up all over her head. She had listened to the whole story, helping me along with a few pats on my arm, and was now trying desperately to convince me that the two of us could undo Maude's spell.

"What?" I stared at her, still gulping from all the tears I'd shed. "She won't undo it, Wanda, she won't. If you'd seen her when she told me what was going to happen you'd believe me."

Wanda wiped the back of her hand across her fore-

128

head. "Why don't we go on back to my house and have something cold to drink? Maybe if we could just cool off, we could think better."

We walked slowly through the woods. By the time we got to Wanda's, we were so hot our T-shirts were clinging to our backs. Annabelle glanced up from one of Charlene's old fashion magazines and waved at us.

"You two look like you're half dead from the heat. Just sit down right here on the steps and I'll bring you each a nice cold glass of fresh lemonade." Leaving her magazine, she went inside.

Without a word, we collapsed on the steps and stared glumly across the yard. When Annabelle reappeared with the lemonade, we drank it slowly, letting the cold liquid fill our mouths and trickle down our throats.

"Hoooo," Annabelle sighed. "Nothing like a cold drink on a hot day. I sure hope we get some rain from those clouds." She pointed at a line of tall, full-bellied clouds drifting slowly along the horizon. "They look like thunderheads in the making." Hitching up her flowered dress, she stretched out her legs. "Excuse my bare legs, but it's just too damned hot for modesty."

I stared at Annabelle's legs spreading out from her hips like soft white hams. Stencilled with clusters of purple veins, loose and quivery, they looked old and sad next to Wanda's and my hard, skinny legs. I felt uncomfortable looking at them and I wished she'd pull her dress down again, heat or no heat.

"Well, well, there goes Maude." Annabelle pointed at the old woman creeping slow as a turtle past the house, her neck extended, her head turning to look at us. She lifted her walking stick and smiled at us and I drew back against Annabelle, shuddering.

"What's the matter, honey? She been bothering you?"

Annabelle put her arm around me and gave me a quick hug. "Just stay away from her and she won't hurt you."

"Do you think she's got evil powers?" Wanda asked.

Annabelle stared after Maude. "Like I told you the other night, there's lots of things in this world I don't know about and that old woman's one of them. I used to go to her and have my fortune told. Sometimes what she said happened and sometimes it didn't. The last time I went to see her, she said I was going to have four more kids to raise and I laughed in her face. Hell, I was forty-five years old and a widow with no hope of finding a husband any time soon. But the very next week, along comes your mother with you four kids. And in another six months she was gone and there I was raising you all."

Annabelle laughed till her thighs shook. "After that, I didn't want any more fortunes told. Sometimes it's better not to know what life's got in store for you."

"But do you think she can cast spells and make bad things happen to people?" Wanda persisted.

"You mean like a witch in a fairy tale?" Annabelle frowned. "I've heard people say she's capable of causing all kinds of trouble. Twyla for one. The last time she was here, she told me to keep you girls away from her, but I don't know. Maude seems harmless to me."

"What does Twyla know about Maude?" Wanda asked.

"Oh, a few years ago, Twyla started hanging around with Maude. There were rumors she was learning witchcraft. She always was a funny little thing, even as a child, so it might have been true." Annabelle paused and lit a cigarette. Exhaling slowly, she added, "Anyway, she and Maude had some sort of a disagreement and Twyla left town. Went all the way to Harrisburg just to get away from her."

Annabelle heaved herself up from the steps and smoothed her dress over her hips. "Much as I hate to drive in this heat, I've got to go into Harrisburg to run some errands. You two want to ride along with me? I bet Laura would enjoy seeing Twyla's shop. It's real cute the way she's got it fixed up."

The two of us jumped up, ready to hop into the car immediately, but Annabelle frowned at Wanda's feet. "You go right inside, Wanda Louise, and get some shoes on. I don't want you stepping on cigarette butts and burning your bare feet." Then she looked at me. "We'll stop by your aunt's so you can get shoes on and ask her if it's all right for you to go."

While Annabelle and Wanda waited in the car, I ran up the back steps and into the kitchen. Aunt Grace was standing at her drawing table, staring at a sketch of a rabbit so stiffly posed I could hardly believe she'd drawn it. Other pencil sketches littered the work surface—squirrels, rocks, ferns, birds, all drawn on paper worn thin with erasing, all as poorly drawn as the rabbit. While I watched, Aunt Grace tore the rabbit in half and crumpled the paper into a ball. As she tossed it into the trash can, she looked up and saw me standing in the doorway.

"What's wrong?" I whispered.

Aunt Grace looked at me, her eyes bright with tears. "I don't know. Nothing looks right to me today. My pictures seem so ordinary, so mediocre, not worth the effort it takes to produce them!"

Sitting down at the table, she buried her face in her

hands, looking more like Mom than herself. "How could I have fooled myself all these years, thinking I was an artist?" Her voice was muffled by her hands and full of tears.

I stared at Aunt Grace, frightened. Timidly I touched her shoulder. "Annabelle invited me to drive to Harrisburg with her and Wanda. Is it all right if I go?"

Aunt Grace nodded her head. "Go on, Laura, and have a nice time." She looked up and smiled at me. "Artists often have bad days. It's probably all the worry about Jason that's making me feel so bad about everything. By the time you get back, I'll try to be feeling more like myself."

"You're sure you'll be all right?" I asked.

Aunt Grace nodded. "Don't worry about me."

"Where's Carol?"

"Out in the yard somewhere taking a sunbath."

I hesitated a minute, then ran up to my room to get my shoes. When I came back down Aunt Grace was still sitting there, bent over her drawing table. Her face looked drawn and tired.

"Annabelle's waiting for me in the car," I said, edging toward the door.

"Well, go on, then, Laura. The poor woman must be roasting like an Easter ham in this heat."

Giving Aunt Grace one last, worried look, I left the house and climbed into the back seat of Annabelle's old Dodge Dart.

chapter

‹14›

"**T**wyla's shop is just about in the middle of this block." Annabelle drew up at a stop sign and pointed down a street lined with old stone buildings. "You two can get out here and I'll go tend to my business. I'll meet you in an hour or so."

Wanda shoved open her door and we climbed out of the car. While we waited to cross the street, I watched Annabelle maneuver her way down the narrow street, swerving around a pickup truck and slowing to let a woman pushing a stroller cross in front of her. As the car swung widely around a corner and disappeared without a mishap, Wanda and I crossed the street.

We passed a small grocery store announcing unadvertised specials on applesauce and tuna fish, a used clothing store with a window full of tired mannequins wearing faded dresses, sequined jackets and mangy fur wraps, an antique shop spilling tables, chairs and bureaus onto the sidewalk, and Jo'Mar's Beauty Salon, perfuming the hot air with the pungent odors of permanents and hair dyes.

"There it is." Wanda pointed at a sign hanging over

a narrow doorway. On it were an owl and a cat in a small green boat. "The Owl and the Pussycat," Wanda said, squinting up at the sign.

"That's from a poem," I said. Seeing Wanda's blank look, I recited, " 'The owl and the pussycat went to sea in a beautiful pea-green boat.' " I paused, trying to remember what came next. "Then there's something about a runcible spoon and a piggy wig with a ring in the end of his nose and they get married by the light of the silvery moon." Wanda looked so perplexed I couldn't help laughing. "Daddy used to read it to me when I was little. It was his favorite poem."

Wanda opened the door and a bell jangled as we entered. Inside it seemed very dark after the bright sunlight and we stood still for a minute, letting our eyes get used to the dim light. The walls of the small shop were lined with floor to ceiling shelves stocked with all sorts of things: hand-thrown pottery, apple-headed dolls, papier-mâché puppets, hand-dipped candles, stuffed animals, batik T-shirts, wooden toys, and hand-woven shawls. From the ceiling hung ceramic wind chimes tinkling in the breeze from an overhead fan, driftwood mobiles turning gracefully, and silent dolls with white satin wings and long yarn hair and beautiful dreamy faces, swaying gently to and fro.

"May I help you?" Behind a counter in one corner, a woman with long blonde hair smiled at us. She was holding an unfinished angel doll in one hand, and the work table beside her was covered with parts of dolls and their costumes. "Or are you just admiring my Sisters of the Moon?"

We looked at each other, neither one of us knowing what she was talking about.

"The dolls, the ones with wings." She held up one. "They're called the Sisters of the Moon."

"They're beautiful." I reached up and touched the silky fabric of the doll's dress.

"Is Twyla here?" Wanda asked, ignoring the dolls.

"She's in the back room reading Tarot cards for a customer. Do you want to talk to her?" The woman smiled at us, her face kind and gentle.

"If she's not too busy," I said.

"She should be finished in a few minutes. You all can look around the shop or just sit down and wait." The woman pointed to a bench under the window.

Wanda walked over and sat down while I watched the woman stuff the doll's body. "Did you make up the pattern for her?"

She nodded. "Twyla thought up the idea and I came up with the pattern. They're one of the most popular things we sell."

Before I could ask any more questions, the beaded curtains covering a doorway behind the counter clattered aside, and a middle-aged woman stepped into the shop. Twyla followed her, looking even more exotic than she had the last time I'd seen her. She had divided her hair into dozens of long, beaded braids, each one smaller in diameter than a baby's finger, and she glittered with bracelets, rings, necklaces and earrings.

"Well, Mrs. Tanenger," she was saying, "you've got to remember that the Hanged Man can represent many things, not all of them bad. I truly think his presence is a positive sign." Her voice was soft and rich, like hot coffee with whipped cream on top.

"I hope you're right, Twyla." Mrs. Tanenger didn't look convinced. While the Sisters of the Moon spun around her, gently nudging her broad shoulders with their tiny hands and pointed toes, she reached out and squeezed Twyla's hand, totally engulfing it with her large one. Then, without looking at Wanda or me, she left the shop.

As I put out a hand to still one of the dolls, swinging wildly in Mrs. Tanenger's wake, Twyla looked at me and smiled.

"Wanda and Laura, what a nice surprise!" Twyla reached out and gave our hands a quick squeeze. "Is Annabelle with you?"

Wanda shook her head. "She's doing some errands, so she brought us in to see your shop."

Twyla smiled. "Did you just want to look around or did you want to see me?"

"Well, we kind of wanted to talk to you about something," Wanda said.

Twyla smiled as if she thought we wanted our fortunes told. She led us through the beaded curtains and into a small room, dimly lit by sunlight shining through two windows set deeply in thick stone walls. A huge fireplace dominated one wall and the other walls were hung with dozens of small mirrors in carved wood frames. Plants of all shapes and sizes hung from the ceiling, clustered on the window sills, and nestled in the corners.

Gesturing at a heap of large, brightly colored pillows heaped around a low table, Twyla told us to sit down. I glanced at the Tarot cards scattered across the table top and shuddered at the sight of the Hanged Man. No matter what Twyla had told Mrs. Tanenger, he looked like bad news to me.

Twyla glanced from Wanda to me, and when neither

of us said anything, she asked about Wanda's family. Especially Tanya Marie.

Wanda hesitated, looking at me first to see if I was going to say anything. "Charlene took her off to Wheeling with Eddie," she finally said, immediately turning her attention to one of her many mosquito bites.

Twyla looked surprised. "You mean after all her begging me to help her, he came back all by himself?" Twyla's bracelets jingled as she reached for the Tarot Cards. Scooping them up, she straightened the deck and set it down on the polished surface of the table.

"Well, not exactly by his self." Wanda turned her attention to the fringe on one of the pillows and began twisting it around her fingers.

"She didn't go to Maude, did she?" Twyla stared so intently at Wanda that she finally looked up at her, her face flushed.

"Yes, she did, that's just what she did," Wanda said.

"Why didn't you help Charlene?" I stared at Twyla.

Twyla frowned. "I told her she was better off without Eddie. Letting him get her pregnant was bad enough, but marrying him would have been much worse. No, I told her to be glad he was gone. But she wouldn't listen to me." Twyla shook her head and her braids swung, clinking beads.

"He didn't act very nice the day he come to get her," Wanda said. "And Annabelle said almost exactly what you said. She didn't want her to go."

"Maude doesn't care about happiness." Twyla stood up and walked to the window. Picking up the Siamese cat lying there, she stroked him gently. With her back to us, she said, "We're going to have a storm tonight. I can feel it coming." Then she added, without turning away from the window, "But you didn't come here about Charlene. You've been to Maude yourselves. Haven't you?" She turned around then, gazing at me over the cat's head.

I shivered and nodded my head. Taking a deep breath, I told her about my parents and how Maude had promised to help me. "But it didn't happen the way I thought it would," I added and told her what Maude had said when I'd seen her in the woods. "What can I do?" I whispered. "Can you help me?"

Twyla's face was full of concern as she crossed the room and sat down next to me. "I knew about Maude and your grandmother. That's why I told Annabelle to keep you and Wanda away from her, but I guess I didn't make my warning strong enough." She patted my hand. "I hope I can help you, but I'm not sure. Maude and I didn't part on the best of terms. She hasn't got much liking for me, nor I for her."

Twyla stroked the cat silently while I watched her face, hoping I'd see a hint of what she was thinking about. But she kept her head bent over the cat, as if she were listening to secrets in his purr.

"Please help me," I whispered, staring at her through a film of tears. "I'm so scared that Jason will never get well and it will be all my fault."

At last she looked up, a frown creasing her forehead. "I'll do almost anything to break one of Maude's spells—no matter what the risk."

Frightened, I stared at her pale face. My heart was pounding so fast, I pressed my hand against my chest, feeling I had to slow it down, keep it from bursting loose. "What do you have to do?"

"First, I have to think of a way to get Maude out of

her house." Twyla stared past us and the room filled with silence. A fly buzzed against the window, cars swooshed by outside, somewhere a siren wailed, but all these sounds seemed far away as if life were going on someplace else without us.

Finally Twyla looked up. "There are things Maude never taught me, things I didn't want to learn. She told me the last time I saw her that I'd be sorry, that someday I'd come crawling back to her, begging her to teach me all she knew. What I have to do is convince her that she was right, that I need her help."

"Will she believe you?" I whispered.

Twyla nodded. "She's a vain old woman. She'll be so delighted her prediction came true that she won't even question my conversion to her way of thinking." Reaching out, she seized my hand. "But I can't do it all by myself, Laura. I'll need your help."

My heart started pounding again and my mouth felt dry with fear. "What can I do?"

"You'll have to get the things you gave Maude."

"Go into her house?"

Twyla nodded. "I'll get her to leave with me and while she's gone you'll have to go inside and get the box."

"All by myself?" I didn't dare look at Wanda. I was sure she wouldn't go.

There was a brief silence and then Wanda said, "I'll go with you, Laura. I want Jason to get well too."

As relief surged through me, Twyla smiled at us. "It will be all right. I'm sure of it. Can you meet me tonight in the grove?"

"Where the path goes up to Maude's house?" I asked.

Twyla nodded. "At eleven-thirty, rain or no rain." She

stood up, still holding the cat, just as the young blonde woman parted the curtains and thrust her head into the room.

"Mrs. Linton is here for the girls," she said.

"Tell her we'll be right out." Twyla squeezed my hand. "Now try not to worry. Be at the tree tonight, storm or no storm."

As we passed through the curtain, Annabelle smiled at us. "Well, what did you all do, go and get your fortunes told?" She winked at Twyla. "I hope you tell better ones than Maude does," she said.

"The future's the future, no matter who sees it," Twyla said, "but I always try to see the best in what's revealed to me." She smiled.

"Well, it's nice to see you, Twyla. Hope these two didn't take up too much of your time. They'll talk your ears off if you let them." Annabelle poked a Sister of the Moon and watched her spin. "Ain't you a darling," she said to the doll and then reached out for Wanda and me. "Come on you two. Got to get on home and get some supper started. It's getting on to six already."

We followed her out the door, listening to the bell chime behind us.

On the way home, Wanda asked Annabelle if I could spend the night with her.

"Well, sure, it's fine with me. Let's just stop by Laura's house again and make sure it's all right with her aunt."

As we drove up, I saw Aunt Grace sitting on the front steps. Jumping out of the car, I ran across the grass.

"Is everything all right?" I asked, stricken with worry that Jason might have gotten worse while I was gone.

Aunt Grace squeezed my hand. "Your mother called

a few minutes ago. They've put Jason in Intensive Care. His fever's way up and he's in terrible pain." Her eyes filled with tears and she let them spill over and run down her cheeks without bothering to brush them away. "I just don't understand why the hospital can't do more for him."

"He'll get well, I know he will." Holding her hand as tightly as I could, I wanted to tell her about Maude and how I was going to take care of everything, but I knew I couldn't. She would never let me go to Maude's house, she would never believe that Maude had anything to do with Jason's being in the hospital.

"How's the little boy?" Annabelle walked across the lawn, her big face full of worry. "He's not worse, is he?"

"He's a little worse." Aunt Grace stood up and put her arm around me, holding me close.

"Oh, I'm so sorry, Grace. Is there anything I can do to help?" Annabelle patted Aunt Grace's shoulder.

"It's kind of you to offer." Aunt Grace smiled and shook her head.

"Well, how about letting me take this one home with me for the night? Give you one less thing to worry about." Annabelle ruffled my hair.

Aunt Grace looked at me. "Would you like to go over to Annabelle's?"

"If it's all right with you." I hoped she didn't think I just wanted to forget about Jason and have fun.

Aunt Grace looked a little puzzled, but she smiled at mè. "Go on up and get a change of clothes. If your mother or father wants to talk to you about anything, I'll send them over to Annabelle's.

Leaving her and Annabelle talking softly, I ran up to my room and grabbed a few things. On my way out, I stole a quick look at the drawing table. Everything was in perfect order, but there was no picture pinned to its surface. I'd never seen Aunt Grace let a day go by without at least starting a painting, and I frowned at Thomas lying peacefully in the middle of her drawing board.

"Get off!" I shoved the cat and he got up slowly, looking haughtier than usual, and leapt to the floor, landing with a solid, ungraceful thud.

"Have a good time," Aunt Grace said as I got into the car, "and be sure to thank Annabelle."

I waved to her as the car pulled away, leaving her small and alone, standing in front of the house.

Neither Wanda nor I could eat much dinner, but, luckily for us, Annabelle blamed it on the weather. "When it's this hot, nothing tastes good," she said, taking our plates out to the kitchen. "Come on out here, girls, and help me wash up."

We finished the dishes around eight o'clock and Annabelle went to the back door and stared out into the gathering darkness.

"Looks like a storm's coming for sure," she said. In the distance thunder muttered and lightning flickered low on the horizon. A gust of wind blew through the door, plastering Annabelle's dress against her stomach and thighs. "Maybe it'll clear things off a bit and get rid of all this heat and humidity. We sure could use some rain and a change in the weather." She smiled at us. "You all going to watch some TV with me?"

Wanda and I followed her into the living room. "What's on?" Wanda asked.

"Oh, I was thinking I'd watch that special, the one with all the country singers." Annabelle flicked on the television set and sat down on the couch. "It's got Willie Nelson and Loretta Lynn and Johnny Cash and I don't know who all," she said as Wanda and I sat down next to her.

After an hour of sad songs about men cheating on their wives and wives cheating on their husbands, Wanda and I were ready for bed. Annabelle looked up at us as we left the living room. "Now don't stay up too late talking and laughing, you two," she said. "And, Wanda, I don't want you smoking. I'll smell it for sure, so don't think you can fool me. This house might not look like much, but it's all I got and I sure don't want to see it burned to the ground 'cause some foolish kid didn't know how to put out a cigarette."

"Don't worry, I don't have any cigarettes," Wanda said. "And neither does Laura. But if I did, I got enough sense not to burn the house down. You're the one who's always falling asleep with a cigarette in your hand, not me."

"Now go on to bed, girl. You know that's a downright lie!" Annabelle gave Wanda a playful swat with the *TV Guide* and laughed, showing all her fillings. "Ain't she something?" she asked me.

We both laughed and ran down the hall to Charlene's old room. Wanda had lined all the dolls and animals up against one wall, so they looked as if they were waiting for a firing squad, but she'd left all of Charlene's posters up. Rock stars, movie stars and fuzzy baby animals stared down at us, all crowded together and billowing a little in the breeze blowing through the window.

"Well, here we are, planning how to sneak out again," Wanda said, flopping down on the bed.

143

"It's a little after ten. Do you think Annabelle's going to bed before eleven?" I sat down next to Wanda and folded my arms across my chest.

"I don't think so. She usually stays up pretty late."

"Then how are we going to get out?"

"Through the window, the way Charlene always did when she wanted to sneak off with Eddie."

"Won't Annabelle hear us?"

"Not with the TV on and all that thunder. All we got to do is turn off the light and stick some of these animals under the sheet. The most she ever does is stick her head in, and most of the time she doesn't even do that." Wanda scratched her leg. "What's the matter? You cold?"

I shook my head. "No, I'm scared."

"Me too. There's no telling what that old woman'd do if she caught us in her house."

"You don't have to go with me, Wanda," I whispered, afraid to look at her. "I'm the one who started all this mess, not you, so I'll understand if you want to change your mind about going."

"Well, I don't want to go and that's the truth, but I'm not letting you do it all by yourself, so don't say no more about it."

I leaned back against the wall. The wind was blowing louder and the thunder sounded a lot closer. A flash of lightning lit the sky and I heard the patter of raindrops on the leaves outside the window. "It's raining," I said.

"It figures," Wanda said gloomily.

As the rain fell harder, we heard Annabelle moving around the house, shutting windows and closing doors.

"You girls got any windows open in there?" she called.

"No, ma'am," Wanda answered, watching Charlene's lacy curtains billow in the wind.

"Well, I'm going to bed. Makes me nervous to watch TV with all that thunder and lightning. You two get to sleep at a decent hour, you hear?"

We heard Annabelle go into her room and shut the door. The bedsprings creaked and then all was silent except for the wind and the thunder.

"It's time to go," Wanda said after a while. Grabbing a baseball jacket, she turned out the light and slid the screen up. "Be real quiet, cause she might not be asleep yet."

I nodded and followed Wanda out the window, pulling up the hood of my windbreaker as soon as the rain hit me. By the time we got to the grove, we were soaked to the skin and shivering.

"Well, where is she?" Wanda swept the trees with her flashlight, but we saw no sign of Twyla.

"She'll be here, she promised," I whispered.

"A car's coming!" Wanda pushed me off the road and we huddled behind a tree, not wanting to be seen. As the car slowed to a stop, I recognized the daisies painted on its sides. Before Twyla had a chance to open the door, Wanda and I were at the window, telling her how glad we were to see her.

"Did you think I wasn't coming?" Twyla gave us each a hug. "A little rain never stopped me. Come on." She led us up the path, twisting and turning through the trees. When we were near Maude's cabin, Twyla drew us under the shelter of a tall, tilted boulder. "I telephoned Maude a few hours ago and convinced her that I need her help. We'll be away from the cabin for about an hour. Do you think you'll be able to find the box?"

I nodded. "I saw her put it under a loose stone on

the hearth, I'm not sure which one, but I know it was on the left side."

"Good. As soon as you find it, take it back to the grove and wait for me. I'll help you destroy it." Reaching into the pocket of her skirt, she pulled out a couple of small bags on red strings. Slipping them over our heads, she said, "Keep these on. They'll protect you against harm."

"It smells funny." Wanda sniffed hers suspiciously. "What is it?"

Twyla smiled. "Don't worry about the smell. Just don't take it off." She darted out into the rain again and we followed her, trying not to slip on the muddy path.

Huddling behind a tree, we watched Twyla run across the clearing. As she knocked at Maude's door, a flash of lightning illuminated the scene, burning it into my brain. The cabin, every board visible; Twyla's small form, her black hair flying loose in the wind, her fist raised to knock; the trees around the cabin tossing against the sky; the door opening and Maude's bent figure silhouetted against the firelight behind her.

As Twyla stepped inside, the lightning died away and we stared at the cabin barely visible in the darkness.

chapter

~<15>~

"Suppose Maude won't go with Twyla because of the rain?" Wanda whispered, her eyes fixed on the cabin door.

I tried to toss the hair out of my face, but it clung to my lips, my nose, my cheeks, plastered there by the rain. "She has to, she told Twyla she would," I answered, praying for the cabin door to open.

Wanda shoved her hands deeper into the pockets of her basball jacket and hunched her shoulders against the rain. Peering around the trunk of the tree, she drew back suddenly. "They're coming!"

Sure enough, there was Twyla running ahead and Maude shuffling along behind her, swathed in shawls and leaning heavily on her walking stick. They passed so close to us that I could have reached out and tweaked the edge of Maude's shawl, but the storm hid us, making it impossible to see anything clearly.

When I was sure they were far enough away, I motioned to Wanda and we ran across the muddy clearing, slipping and sliding on the rain-washed ground. At the bottom of the steps, I stopped so suddenly that Wanda ran into me.

"What's the matter?" she whispered, her voice shaking.

I looked at her, my mouth dry with fright.

"You scared?"

"Aren't you?" This close to the house, I could smell wood smoke from the chimney, mingling with the strange fragrances of herbs and incense and underneath them, the unpleasant scent of worse things, decay and mold and rot and death.

"You want to save Jason, don't you?" Stepping ahead of me, Wanda tiptoed up the sagging steps and pushed the door open with a trembling hand. "Come on, Laura, we ain't got much time," she whispered.

Hesitating on the threshold, I could feel the warmth of the fire burning low on the hearth, but the flickering shadows and strange smells, the very atmosphere of the room, suggested that Maude was hiding somewhere, ready to pounce upon us. Behind us a gust of wind struck our shoulders, shaking the cabin and rattling the windows, breathing new life into the flames, almost propelling us into the cabin. Cautiously we crept to the fireplace, aware of the stuffed owl on the mantel regarding us with glassy eyes.

"Which stone did she pull out?" Wanda knelt at the hearth, examining the pattern of the stones.

"This one, I think." As I reached for the stone, something above my head moved suddenly and I sprang back, finding myself staring into the eyes of Maude's crow.

Like an explosion of darkness, Soot flew at me, his wings beating against the sides of my head. Fending him off with my hands, I ducked aside and Soot flew past me, cawing loudly. Too late, I saw that we'd left the door open, permitting him to fly out into the storm.

"He'll go to Maude!" I began pulling frantically at stones, trying to find the box before Maude came back. "Help me, Wanda!"

Wanda crouched next to me, her fingers scrabbling at the stones, poking, prying, pulling. "This one feels loose," she panted. "Help me with it!"

As I grabbed the stone, I heard someone on the steps. Terrified, I whirled around and saw Maude, the crow perched on her shoulder.

"So!" Maude rushed toward us, her dark clothes fluttering around her like a crow's feathers, her face twisted with rage. Before I could do more than stand up, she seized me, her nails biting into my arm as she shook me. "What are you doing here?"

"Maude!" Twyla rushed into the room, pale and wet. "Let them go!"

Maude stared at Twyla without relaxing her grip on either one of us. "What are they to you? Did you come here with this in mind, Twyla? Wasn't one betrayal enough?"

Twyla stepped closer to Maude, tiny and thin and brave, her eyes black with anger. "You know how I feel about you and your spells. Let these girls go now and forget about the past."

"You are still the ignorant young fool you used to be, Twyla Dawkins!" Maude's voice rose and she herself seemed to grow taller, to swell with rage till her shadow blackened the ceiling. "If I could I would strip you of all the knowledge I gave you. I would send you out into the night as helpless as a newborn kitten, blind and deaf, too feeble to survive the storm. I would curse you and loose the hounds of the Master against you!"

Maude sank down, but her grip on Wanda and me never slackened. "But I'm not what I was and you know it." Her voice was low now, almost a whisper, but so full of malice that I shivered.

"Let the girls go, Maude." Twyla's voice was calm. She stood still, unmoved by Maude's fury.

Maude shook her head and pulled me closer to her. "Perhaps I'll let one go." She smiled at Wanda. "But not this one, not Margaret Randall's granddaughter. She is mine now, mine, and she will stay with me. Won't you, my dear?" Thrusting her face close to mine, she whispered, "You liked me well enough when you wanted my help, didn't you, Laura Adams? And you can't say I didn't grant your wish, can you?"

I tried to turn my head away, but Maude released Wanda and gripped my chin, forcing me to look at her. This close, Maude's face was pocked with pores, dark hairs sprouted above her lip and lined her nostrils, deep furrows creased her cheeks and forehead, and hundreds of tiny lines crisscrossed the skin around her eyes. The fingers gripping my chin were cold and rough, and her nails gouged my skin. Tears filled my eyes, blurring her face, and my knees felt too weak to support me.

Out of the corner of my eye, I saw Wanda run to Twyla's side and cower there. Embracing Wanda, Twyla stared coldly at Maude. "Let Laura go too, Maude."

"She is mine, I tell you, mine!" Maude's voice rose again and she shook me roughly. "Look at me, girl, look at me! Do you doubt my power over you?"

As I stared at her, terrified, Maude seemed to tower above me, a creature of malice dressed in black, full of power and hatred, and I felt totally helpless. There was nothing I could do against her. She was right. I was hers, hers. If she hadn't been holding me so tightly, I would have fallen to the floor.

"You're wasting your time, Maude Blackthorne." Twyla stared calmly at the old woman. "Look at her neck. She has the amulet's protection. As long as she's wearing that, you cannot harm her."

Maude drew in her breath sharply as she looked at the little pouch hanging on its red ribbon. Gripping me even tighter, she turned to Twyla. "Take that one with you." She pointed at Wanda. "But give this one to me. You owe me something in return for all I've taught you." Maude's voice was wheedling now, but she still held me tightly.

Twyla shook her head. "Let her go, Maude."

Maude stared hard at Twyla and Twyla stared back, neither blinking nor looking away. While they stared at each other, I saw Wanda slip away and return to the hearth. Taking advantage of Twyla's and Maude's silent battle, she struggled to loosen the stone. As I watched, I saw her pull the stone noiselessly up and reach into the hole.

When she removed the small metal box, Soot cawed loudly, but no one paid any attention to him. The eyes of the two women seemed locked together and the tension between them silenced every sound.

With one arm upraised to protect herself against Soot, who was beating her head with his wings, Wanda ran back to Twyla's side, hiding the box behind her.

At that moment, Twyla shouted something in a strange language, a curse, an order, something harsh and terrible to hear, and Maude, momentarily startled, loosened her grip on me. Breathless with fear, I ran to Twyla's side.

"Go!" Twyla shouted to me and Wanda. "Meet me

where I told you to!" With her arms outstretched she began chanting, never taking her eyes from Maude, and Maude seemed to freeze, unable to follow me.

"Traitor!" she screamed at Twyla. "To use against me what I myself taught you!"

Without looking back, Wanda and I ran from the cabin. Heedless of the branches slapping us and tangling in our hair, we dashed through the woods, ducking, dodging, tripping, hearts pounding, lungs bursting. Finally we reached the grove and ran to Twyla's car. Clinging to each other, shivering with fear and cold, we stared up the path, hoping to see Twyla come running toward us. The rain had almost stopped and the thunder had died away to a distant rumble.

"Here she comes!" Wanda grabbed my arm and pointed as Twyla ran out of the woods. Although I expected to see Maude pursuing her, she was alone. There was no sign of the old woman.

"Give me the things," Twyla gasped.

Wanda thrust the box into Twyla's outstretched hand, as if it were burning her.

"Stand back," Twyla said.

As she broke the threads that were sealing the box shut, I recognized them for what they were: strands of my own hair. Shuddering, I remembered the times Maude had stroked my hair, running her fingers through it till it had hurt. She had been pulling out strands of it to use in the spell.

Removing a box of matches from her pocket, Twyla ignited the contents of the box. A tall flame rose, illuminating Twyla's face with blue light. She drew a circle in the earth, set the box down within it, and seized our hands. Chanting, she led us around the circle, using words in a language I'd never heard.

The flame rose, taller and taller, bathing us all in blue light. Looking into its depths, I thought I could see all the things Maude had predicted for us quivering there. Then, as quickly as it had flared up, the flame shrank and went out, leaving the three of us standing, hand in hand, in ordinary darkness.

For the first time that night, Twyla smiled. Giving our hands a quick squeeze, she released us. "I think it will be all right now," she said softly.

Throwing my arms around her, I burst into tears and Twyla held me, letting me cry, stroking my hair, murmuring comforting sounds, until her voice and the wind in the trees blended together like a lullabye and I relaxed.

"Come." Twyla lifted my face and kissed my cheeks and wiped my nose with a handkerchief. "It's all right now, Laura, it's all right. The spell is broken."

"But it was all my fault." I felt tears fill my eyes again.

Twyla shook her head. "Maude took advantage of your unhappiness, Laura. It was natural for you to want your parents to stay married, to want to go home, to want your life to stay the same. You didn't know Maude's price, you didn't know her terms. You mustn't blame yourself for wanting your parents to love each other." Twyla hugged me. "Wanting love isn't wicked, Laura, but sometimes it can lead to wickedness."

Putting her arm around my shoulders, Twyla led us to the car. "Come on, let's get you two home before we all catch pneumonia."

"But what about Maude?" Wanda asked as we drove up the road. "What happened to her?"

Twyla shook her head. "You don't need to worry about Maude any more. Forget her."

"Did lightning strike her house and burn her up?" Wanda grinned at me, obviously relishing the idea.

Twyla smiled. "No, nothing that dramatic happened, Wanda." She paused a moment to push her damp hair out of her eyes. "Let's just say that Maude has been more or less defused. I really don't want to talk about it. You'll understand the next time you see her, Wanda."

Wanda and I looked at each other, trying to understand what Twyla meant. I remembered that Maude had wanted to strip Twyla of her powers but hadn't the strength to do it. Had Twyla possessed that sort of strength? Mystified, I pressed a little closer to her side, grateful for her protection.

By the time we got to Wanda's house, I was exhausted. With a boost from Twyla, the two of us climbed through Wanda's window. Waving good-bye, we watched Twyla slip away down the hillside, without even rousing the dogs, and drive off into the darkness.

"You sure look a sight," Wanda said, staring at me in the soft glow from Charlene's little lamp.

"I couldn't look any worse than you do." As quietly as possible, we tiptoed into the bathroom, cleaned up as best we could, and crept back to bed.

Although Wanda fell asleep almost at once, I lay awake for a long time, worrying about Jason and my parents and Aunt Grace. I was almost afraid for morning to come. Suppose I went home and found everything exactly the same?

chapter

◄16►

The morning sun woke me, but I lay still for a few minutes, waiting for Wanda to show some signs of life. As soon as she stirred, I bent over her and whispered, "Are you awake?"

Wanda screwed up her face and shook her head. "Uh uh, not yet. It's too early to wake up."

"I've got to go home, I've got to see if everything's all right." I got out of bed and groped around the floor for my clothes. My T-shirt was still damp and my shorts were crusty with mud, but I pulled them on anyway.

"My lord, you look like you tangled with a bobcat in a pigpen," Wanda said. "You got scratches all over you. What's your aunt going to think?"

"Maybe she won't notice."

"Maybe. If she's got her eyes closed, that is." Wanda got out of bed and pulled on a pair of overalls and a T-shirt. "Come on, let's get something to eat. I feel half-starved from not eating anything last night. Don't you?"

I shrugged. "I'll probably feel hungrier after I know Jason's better."

Out in the kitchen, Annabelle was having a cup of

155

coffee and singing along with the radio. "Well, that storm really cleared the air, didn't it? It's just beautiful this morning, the best-looking day I seen in a long time." She smiled out the window at the blue sky as if she'd polished it herself. "Even the birds sound happier," she added.

"What's for breakfast? I'm half dead from starvation." Wanda sat down at the table and looked at Annabelle.

"Well, there's coffee, fresh made, and cereal and toast." Annabelle looked at us, noticing our appearance for the first time. "You all look awful. How'd you get all scratched up like that? Did you go out in that storm last night?"

"Well, just a little. We couldn't sleep, Annabelle." Wanda grinned at her grandmother and took the bowl of cereal she offered her. "Bananas on top! You just think of everything."

Annabelle smiled. "Well, don't go out in no more storms like that. You could've been struck by lightning and then what would I have told Grace Randall?"

When I'd eaten enough breakfast to satisfy Annabelle, I got up to go home.

"I'll walk with you," Wanda said, leaving Annabelle happily washing dishes and singing a sad song about a no-good boy who ran away from home and broke his mother's heart.

Outside the air was fresh and clean, just as Annabelle had said, and we walked together down the road, talking about Maude and wondering what Twyla had done to her. When we got to the edge of the grove, we paused and looked at each other, then peered ahead of us into the shade.

"I don't see her," Wanda whispered. "But I hear a crow."

"So do I. What should we do? The only other way to my house is down by the creek and we'd still have to pass the path to her house."

"We could hold hands and run through." Wanda put a finger in her mouth and chewed at her nail.

"Okay. I'll get my aunt or somebody to drive you home, so you won't have to come back by yourself." I reached out for her hand and we ran down the hill and into the grove.

The road was muddy and cool from the rain and the air smelled of wet moss, damp bark, and moist earth. Bursting out again into the sunshine, I took a deep breath and laughed. "Not a sign of her!"

"Maybe she's dead, like in *The Wizard of Oz*. Twyla just melted her away."

Singing "Ding Dong, the Wicked Witch is Dead," we ran up the lawn to Aunt Grace's house, almost dizzy with excitement.

We found Aunt Grace in the kitchen, bent over her drawing board, sketching a grove of trees outside the window. When she saw us, she sprang up, her face happy. "Oh, Laura, I have good news!" She nearly swept me off my feet with a big hug. "Jason is better this morning, much better! Your mother called about an hour ago."

I hugged her back as hard as I could. "When can I go see him?"

"As soon as you can get ready." Aunt Grace drew back and smiled at me, then looked puzzled. "How on earth did you get so scratched up? You look as if you fell in a briar patch."

I looked down at my scarred legs and shrugged. "Wanda and I went for a walk last night. I guess we sort of wandered off the path."

"You weren't out in that storm, were you?"

"Just a little."

"Well, no harm done. Go on upstairs and change your clothes. We'll go as soon as you're ready."

"Can we drop Wanda off at her house on the way?"

"Of course." Aunt Grace smiled at Wanda. "Would you like a cup of coffee while we wait?"

Wanda nodded and looked at the picture on the drawing board. "It sure is nice seeing you painting again. I just love the way you draw."

Aunt Grace smiled. "I was sitting at the table having my first cup of coffee and the light was so pretty on the trees, I just had to paint them. I'm glad you like it."

Leaving them in the kitchen, I ran upstairs. As I reached the bathroom door, Carol stepped out. She was enveloped in a cloud of warm steamy air and smelled of shampoo and soap and conditioner.

"Isn't it wonderful about Jason?" she said. "I've been so worried about that little guy." Carol shook her head. "And your poor Daddy, it's been an awful strain on him. Are you going to see him?"

"As soon as I get cleaned up."

Carol stepped away from the door and smiled. "Well, the bathroom's all yours. Hope you don't mind it all steamy, but I just love long, hot showers. All that water feels so good, opens your pores, lets your skin breathe."

I nodded and closed the bathroom door, hoping she'd left enough hot water to open my pores a little.

When I came downstairs, Aunt Grace and Wanda were finishing up a sinkful of dishes and chatting like old friends. "Ready?" Aunt Grace asked.

158

After dropping Wanda off, we drove into Harrisburg and parked in front of the hospital, a rambling old frame building that looked like a turn-of-the-century hotel, enlarged with brick additions and bristling with fire escapes.

Inside we wandered down miles of brown linoleum hallways, past door after door of sick people watching us go by. Some had flowers by their beds, some had dozens of get-well cards stuck in their venetian blinds, and some were just lying there, looking sad and lonely as if they hoped we were coming to see them. I didn't want to look at them, but I couldn't help it. I peeped in each door, glimpsing people of all ages, and if I didn't see their faces, I saw their bare feet poking out from under sheets.

"Jason's room is just around this corner," Aunt Grace said. "He'll be so pleased to see you, Laura. I know he's missed you."

"You're sure he's better?" I felt my knees getting kind of trembly. I didn't want to see Jason if he looked awful; I wouldn't know what to say, what to do.

"Oh, yes, Laura. He's much better. His fever went down overnight and he says the pain in his legs is all gone. The doctors are absolutely mystified. They've never seen anyone recover as rapidly as Jason has." Aunt Grace smiled at me. "Don't be frightened." She squeezed my hand and led me to Jason's door.

And there he was, sitting up in bed, smiling. "Laurie!" he cried, "Oh, Laurie, I've missed you!" His face was pale and he looked thinner, but his smile was as big as ever.

"Oh, Jasie, Jasie, I've missed you too!" I sank down on the bed and hugged him. "I'm so sorry you've been sick!"

"Now, now, Laura, no tears." Daddy smiled at me from a chair next to Jason's bed. "He's been a brave boy and he's all right now."

Jason smiled. "That's right, Laurie. Even the doctors said how brave I was." He shot Daddy a look and then turned back to me. "Where's Wanda?" He peered around my shoulder as if he expected to see her lurking in the hall.

"She couldn't come, but she said to tell you she's glad you're better. Everybody was worried about you, even Annabelle."

Jason looked pleased. "When I come home, you and me and Wanda can build a great big sand castle. It can have towers and stairs and a moat around it and a dungeon underneath."

"We can build a regular Camelot all our own," I agreed. "And you can be the king, Jason."

"Don't forget this, son." Daddy picked up a brand new football and tossed it to Jason. He missed it, and it landed on his table, knocking his pitcher of water into Mom's lap.

"I'm sorry!" Jason's eyes filled with tears and he looked from Mom to Dad, as if he weren't sure which one he should apologize to.

While Mom blotted up the water with a towel from the bathroom, Daddy retrieved the football. "No need to cry about it," he said. "Just shows you need some practice. As soon as you get home, I'll teach you a few tricks." He ruffled Jason's hair and smiled at me.

"But first of all, the castle," I said firmly. "Because you can't just get out of bed and start playing football and stuff like that." I looked at Daddy out of the corner of my eye, but he didn't say anything. He just sat there tossing the football from one hand to the other as if he were thinking about something else.

Turning back to Jason, I started describing the sort of castle we could build. I guess we spent half an hour planning it, from turrets to dungeon.

Suddenly Jason leaned toward me, his face worried. "But what about Maude, Laurie? She'll see us at the creek."

I shook my head. "She won't come, Jason."

"How do you know?"

"I just know. You don't have to be scared of her."

"What's this about Maude?" Mom looked up from her magazine. "Did she scare you, Jason?"

Jason glanced at me, remembering his promise not to mention Maude. "She's a scary old lady." He picked at the fuzz balls on his blanket, his face hidden.

Daddy smiled. "Oh, Jason, your imagination carries you away so easily. Next you'll be saying she's a witch."

"She is," Jason whispered so softly only I could hear him. "I know she is."

Just then a nurse came into the room, pushing a cart that tinkled with bottles and test tubes and all sorts of sinister medical things. "Well, it's time to run a few more tests, Jason," the nurse said. "The chief vampire wants some more of your blood."

"Oh, no." Jason lay back on his pillows. "Not again. My arm already looks like a pincushion."

"Everybody out," the nurse said, "unless you like the sight of blood."

"Well, old man," Daddy said, "I think I'll take your sister for a ride. I haven't seen much of her lately."

"But she just got here." Jason stuck out his lip, and for the first time in my life I was glad to see it. More

161

than anything else, that pout said Jason was feeling like himself again.

"I'll see you tomorrow when you come home," I said, giving him a kiss.

Daddy patted Jason's head. "Be good now and don't break this nice young lady's heart."

The nurse giggled and Aunt Grace said, "Leave that to you, right, George?"

Outside the sun was hot, and I winced when my bare legs touched the vinyl seats in the car. As we pulled away from the hospital, Daddy noticed a Dairy Queen down the street. "I could really go for a nice, cold shake, couldn't you?" Turning into the parking lot, he took a space vacated by an old pickup truck full of sunburned teenagers. "What kind do you want?" he asked.

"Usually all they have is vanilla," I said, following him up to the counter.

The girl at the window reminded me of Charlene. She had the same easy smile and slow way of moving as she took our order. Like Charlene, she wore her hair long and winged back from her face, and her cheeks were powdered orangy red. When she handed the shakes to us, she smiled at Daddy.

While he paid for the milkshakes, I wondered if Charlene would come back to Blue Hollow. Now that the spell was broken, maybe she'd see that Eddie wasn't really so hot as a husband and father. It was funny to catch myself thinking that some people might be better off not married to each other, that some kids might be happier not living with their own fathers. I could see now that Wanda had been right when she'd said that she and Annabelle and Charlene were all the family Tanya Marie needed.

As we drove away, I sipped my milkshake, but it was too thick to come through the straw.

"What's the matter? Don't you like your shake?" Daddy asked.

"It's too thick and it's got too much vanilla in it. It burns the back of my throat." Turning my head, I looked out the window for a while, watching the scenery flow by. Fields, hills, mountains, woods, their monotony broken by scatterings of farms and an occasional store or church. And the sky, always the sky, high and clear and blue without a single cloud.

Turning back to Daddy, I looked at his profile. With the wind from the open window ruffling his hair, he looked more like Robert Redford than ever. "Are you and Mom definitely getting a divorce?"

He looked at me, his face puzzled. "I thought you knew we were, Laura. Probably next winter sometime."

"I just wondered if Jason's being sick had changed anything."

He shook his head. "Not really. It's funny though. For a while, when he was in intensive care, we talked about staying married for his sake. He seemed to need us both so badly." He sighed. "But it would have been a mistake. I just don't think we could be happy together, your mother and I. In the long run it would have been bad for all of us."

"But you must have been happy when you first got married, you must have loved each other then. How come it all stopped?"

"People change, honey. Their feelings change too." He looked at me. "I know you're disappointed, Laura, but you've got to accept it, you and Jason both. After all, I'm divorcing your mother, not you. I'll always be your father and I'll always love you. That's one thing that won't ever change."

I nodded and sipped some of my milkshake. It still tasted bitter, as if there were something nasty in it that all the sugar couldn't hide. "Are we going back to Aunt Grace's already?" I asked as Daddy turned off the main road.

"I thought we'd pick up Carol and take her with us. She's probably pretty lonesome in that big house all by herself. You don't mind, do you?"

"I thought you and I were going by ourselves."

"I want you to get to know Carol better, Laura. You'll be seeing a lot of her next fall when you're back home."

I didn't want to ask the next question, but I had to know. "You're going to marry her, aren't you?"

"We're thinking about it, honey. You like Carol, don't you? She thinks you two are just terrific." He smiled. "She's a wonderful girl, she really is."

I looked down at my lap, at my two hands holding the milkshake, not wanting to say anything till I was sure I could do it without crying. "Do you mind if I don't go with you?" I asked without looking at him. "Could you just drop me off at Wanda's house instead?"

"But I was going to take you out to the lake for a swim. Wouldn't you like that?"

"I sort of promised Wanda I'd come over and tell her about Jason as soon as I got home."

Daddy looked disappointed, but he said, "All right, Laura, if that's what you really want to do."

For the next half hour we drove along in silence, and I watched the scenery again, thinking about what

164

Daddy had said. I felt sad, but in a funny way I was also kind of relieved. I could see now that, like it or not, the divorce was out of my hands. There was nothing Jason or I could do to change things.

"How does Mom feel?" I asked suddenly.

"The same way I do, Laura. She seems to be looking forward to finishing school and getting a job. She's changed a lot since we separated last January. Don't you think so?"

I shrugged. "I don't know." But I knew he was probably right. Mom really did seem to be a lot more sure of herself now. Not like Aunt Grace, not that kind of independent, but I didn't think she'd cry into the meatloaf anymore.

"That's Wanda's house, right up there on the hill." I pointed and Daddy slowed the car.

"We'll miss you," he said, as I opened the door. "Sure you won't change your mind?"

"I'll come some other time, I promise." I smiled at him and waved as the car picked up speed and disappeared around a curve. Then I ran up the hill to Wanda's house, ignoring Chief's bark as I passed the truck.

chapter

~17~

Dashing up the steps, I pressed my face against the rusty screen door and peered into the living room. "Wanda?" I called. "Are you home?"

"Come on in," she yelled. "I'm in my room."

Letting the door slam behind me, I ran down the hall and flopped down on the bed next to her. "Guess what? Jason's all right! He's coming home tomorrow! Isn't that great?"

Wanda punched me up and down my arm. "You mean he's all well again?"

I nodded. "Nobody at the hospital knows what was wrong with him. They're calling it one of those mysterious viruses."

"Is that you, Laura?" Annabelle poked her head into the room. "I thought I heard your voice, but I didn't expect to see you back so soon."

"I just got back from the hospital. They're letting Jason come home tomorrow."

"Well, that's just wonderful!" Annabelle bent down and gave me a big perfumy hug that almost broke every rib in my body. "I knew he'd be all right, I just knew it."

Annabelle sank down on the bed, toppling me down-hill into her soft side. "You be sure and bring him up here to see me the minute he's well enough and I'll bake him a big chocolate cake. Never knew a boy who didn't love chocolate!"

Turning to Wanda, Annabelle gave her a little poke. "Did you tell Laura our good news?"

Wanda grinned. "I haven't had a chance. Guess who's coming home?"

"Charlene?"

Wanda nodded. "She called a couple of hours ago to tell us. Her and Tanya Marie are probably on the Greyhound right now."

Annabelle looked at me. "I told Charlene she'd be back, didn't I? Didn't I stand right here in this very room and tell her she could come home any time?"

I nodded.

Annabelle sighed and lit a cigarette. "These young people just don't know what they want these days, and that's a fact. I sure hope you two grow up with more sense than Charlene's got."

"Don't worry," Wanda said, "I ain't ever getting married."

"Me either," I said.

Annabelle blew out a cloud of cigarette smoke and chuckled. "Oh, honey, just 'cause some marriages don't work out doesn't mean they're all bad. While Wanda's grandaddy was alive, you couldn't have found a happier woman than me. I been looking for someone like him for twenty years now, and if I ever find him I'll marry him quicker than a cat can drink a bowl of milk." She hugged me again and heaved herself up from the bed. "How about I fix you all a sandwich?"

After lunch, Wanda got a pack of playing cards and we sat out on the front porch playing Spit. A nice breeze was blowing, rustling the leaves and tossing the heads of the Queen Anne's Lace. Down in the field, a mockingbird was singing and in the woods behind the house a jay called.

While Wanda dealt a new hand of cards, I looked out across the valley at the mountains. Clouds high in the sky were casting moving shadows across the trees, changing their color from green to purply blue and back to green again, and all around us everything seemed quiet and peaceful.

"How about the divorce?" Wanda asked quietly. "What are your parents going to do now?"

I looked down at my cards, staring at the double faces of the Queen of Hearts and the King of Clubs. "They're getting it this winter. I asked Daddy."

"You still upset about it?"

I shrugged. "Sort of. I love them both, you know? It would be so much easier if they lived together."

"Not unless they loved each other."

I nodded. "I know." I watched a tear splash down on the Queen's face. "But they don't—they don't love each other anymore. So I guess they're doing the best thing. I wouldn't want them to live the way Maude said, hating each other, always unhappy."

Wanda's hand touched mine, gave it a little squeeze. "It'll be okay," she said.

"Daddy's probably going to marry Carol," I muttered, not daring to look at her for fear she'd say she told me so.

"She's a jerk," Wanda said.

"I know." I grinned at her. "I hope Daddy finds out before he marries her."

Just as I was about to lose the third game in a row, I saw a cab stop at the foot of the driveway. As Charlene opened the door to get out, Annabelle scooted down the steps, waving and smiling. Wanda and I followed after.

"I thought you was going to call me from the depot," Annabelle said. "You didn't have to go wasting your money on a taxicab."

Charlene brushed her hair out of her face and handed Tanya Marie to her grandmother. "I didn't feel like sitting around Blue Hollow waiting for you." She pulled her suitcase and two cardboard boxes out of the cab. Thrusting the suitcase at Wanda, she burst into tears. "Don't give me no lectures, Annabelle," she sobbed. "You were right and I should've listened to you, so just leave me alone."

Annabelle nestled Tanya Marie on her hip and put her arm around Charlene. "Honey, honey, don't worry. I'm glad you're back, that's all. Now come on up to the house and lie down for a while. You must be all worn out."

Without another word, Charlene followed Annabelle up the driveway, leaving us with the suitcase and boxes.

"Well, she could at least have said hello to me," Wanda said, but she carried the suitcase up the hill and set it on the porch next to the door. "Guess she can haul it the rest of the way when she needs it."

Dumping the boxes next to the suitcase, I looked at Wanda. "Maybe Twyla made that spell wear off too."

"Could be." We stared at each other and I could feel little prickles run up and down the back of my neck. Wanda shivered and hugged herself. "Life is awful strange sometimes, isn't it?"

I nodded and we sat down side by side on the porch

railing, watching the shadows drift across the mountains.

"There's your aunt's car," Wanda said.

As the car swung around the curve and dipped down the hill, I got up. "I guess I'd better go home. It must be almost six o'clock."

"You want me to walk part way with you?"

I shook my head. "There's nothing to be scared of now."

Wanda grinned. "Well, then, I'll see you tomorrow. Maybe we can go down the creek where it's deep enough to swim."

"That sounds like a great idea. Come over tomorrow, okay?" I waved good-bye and ran down the steps. As I passed the truck, Chief stuck out his head and barked, but I smiled at him, keeping a safe distance. "You're not as bad as you'd like to think you are," I said.

Chief made a snuffling sound and crawled back under the truck. Turning around, I waved at Wanda again and started down the road.

When I got near the grove, I hesitated, feeling scared in spite of myself. The late afternoon sun had retreated from the woods and it looked dark and spooky under the trees. Looking around for Maude, I walked slowly into the gloom, feeling my heart thump against my ribs.

Suddenly a crow rose from a branch over my head, cawing loudly. Flinching away from him, I saw Maude step out into the road ahead of me. She stopped and stared at me, leaning on her stick and mumbling, but she made no move toward me. For an immeasurable period of time, we both stood still, watching each other, saying nothing. Finally Maude took a step, her feet shuffling, and stopped again within a foot of me, her eyes probing my face.

"Such a pretty girl," she whispered, reaching out a shaking hand to touch my face, but dropping it less than an inch from my cheek. "Don't I know you? Aren't you Margaret?"

She shook her head, her eyes bewildered. "No, no, you can't be Margaret. That was a long time ago, a long, long time ago. Margaret left me, she went away and left me all alone." Maude sighed. "But you look like her—yes, you look like her."

"Don't you remember me?" I whispered.

"Remember you? Should I remember you?" Maude drew her shawl tightly about herself. "No, no, I don't remember you."

As she stared at me, searching my face for clues, Soot dropped down gently on her shoulder and cawed softly. "Yes, yes, it's time to go, my pretty," Maude whispered to the crow. "Time to go."

"Without looking at me again, Maude stepped around me and hobbled away down the road, talking softly to Soot.

For a few seconds I stood still and stared after her. Then I turned and ran toward my aunt's house.